Praise for

Privilege

"Take a dash of Francine Prose, a dash of Donna Tart and add a third original voice, and you have Thomas Carry's brilliant debut novel, *Privilege*. It is a moving, often disturbing, sometimes humorous tale. Carry writes with black humor about an indolent university professor and his star academic wife whose lives are drastically changed within a three-day period of unexpected mayhem. With clever, skillful plot twists and elegant prose, Carry vividly shows how difficult it can be to understand another person's intentions, and demonstrates how unfeelingly cruel, how profoundly stupid and how disarmingly disingenuous some people can be, even in academia. *Privilege* is a riveting read from a gifted craftsman and true storyteller who knows how to end a story."

—**Ray Carson Russell**, Author of *Philurius College Blues*

"In *Privilege*, Professor Daniel Waite has it all—tenure, well-liked, his classes in film studies full, married to the beautiful shining star of this prestigious university. Yet he has attained a mind-numbing level of apathy and misery. Then his new female TA shows up, and life changes dramatically. Set in the insulated culture of academia, this story grabs the reader early on, moves rapidly through one surprise after another, and gives a whole new meaning to the concept of tenure. The book is most entertaining and oddly disturbing; a bold and exciting new formula for a murder mystery. I look forward to more from Mr. Carry."

—**John J. Jessop**, Author of *Pleasuria: Take As Directed, Guardian Angel: Unforgiven, Guardian Angel: Indoctrination*

Privilege

by Thomas H. Carry

Published by

köhlerbooks™

210 60th Street
Virginia Beach, VA 23451
800–435–4811
www.koehlerbooks.com

PRIVILEGE

A NOVEL

THOMAS H. CARRY

VIRGINIA BEACH
CAPE CHARLES

For Carrie, my parents, and steadfast friends.

Prologue

A freshly dead body at your feet is a real eye-opener. It makes a person take stock, assess life choices, confront long-dormant questions repressed by time and habit. Looking back now, for example, I knew the snap decision to loop the cord tightly around her neck and silence her had its genesis in my lack of desire—my lack of passion for anything, really. Decision? No, that's not quite right. It was more of a rending: a sudden and violent revolution overthrowing my established order. A venal jack-in-the-box, popping out of my heart and gorging on all, screeching like the baby alien in *Alien*—okay, sorry, that's probably too much. Please excuse the hyperbole; I'm new to the confessional genre. You get the picture. It was a big change for me. An odd one, since I was never an overly spirited man. I lacked that flame; I was mostly steady, calm. Some would even say passive, though I think that's taking it too far (especially now).

But lately it had been more than that, this lack. Not specific, sharp in its point, but chronic and encompassing, dull and vague; a wet tent collapsing inward. It also fed a heavy pit of resentment, one I diligently suppressed, heeding to my stoic nature. Was I masking it well? I was pretty sure my students and colleagues were oblivious to my state. I would often compensate with geniality, my raised eyebrows and open face masking my apathy. The students . . . if I'd had the commitment to hate them, I would have. Instead, they simply made me tired. Forty-three years of age, congenitally average in weight, height, and looks, I was an inoffensive man of the comfortable sort. "Danny always calms the room," Abbie, my wife, would say in social gatherings with University colleagues. That always got smiles and nods of recognition. I was like a very pleasant virus, contagious but passing soon. People liked me.

Chapter One

I looked up from my notes and out from the lectern. The room was large, with oak and dusty plaster, sweeping up and back with fourteen inclined rows of twenty wooden chairs. The annoying patter of laptop keyboards drummed whenever I paused to throw out a question or to allow a point to sink in. The late Monday morning light struggled in through stained, drafty windows that rattled from time to time with a chilly mid-September breeze. I had a brief and irrational moment of panic, wondering if I was the actual source of the sour smell in the room—a mix of stale wood, stress perspiration, and cleaning solvents.

My course, Introduction to Film Studies, was a generally popular undergraduate class. Not because of my charismatic teaching or the students' deep love of film history (I was no longer surprised by their film illiteracy, the mostly blank stares when I'd throw out lines from *The Godfather* or *Manhattan*). On the unsanctioned faculty review site, Tweed, students labeled me inoffensive and mildly humorous. *Daniel Waite, Associate Professor of English and Film Studies, is not too hard of a grader. The course screens lots of movies, some even interesting. Moderate workload, a midterm and a final essay.*

Enrollment was robust, most students checking off the humanities requirement box, several taking it as the prerequisite to the film studies major. The latter group could be the most vexing; God, had I been that pretentious as an undergraduate? Foucault discursively coupling with Norman Bates, something about fluidity, intersectionality, and power. This from Gary Fallis, a pompous, bloviating film major, who was droning on to my question about *Psycho*'s opening credits, citing every post-something theorist he'd likely never read.

Yes, I was perhaps touchy on the subject. I'd been obsessed with *Psycho*'s opening since discovering the film as a child, cross-legged in my bedroom, my face peering into the old black-and-white, an oracle of secret worlds to which I had private entry. With no cable connection in my room, the makeshift antenna's shaky reception only added to the otherworldliness, the little screen a looking glass into a silvery land of shimmer and static. I remember first bearing witness to the credit's linear patterns, sliced by those iconic sharp string chords, assembling and disassembling rapidly and madly. The whole landscape of Norman's mind visually told in a tight, manic algorithm, a code I desperately wanted to break.

"The opening sequence *prevents* the gaze of the other, it *marginalizes*. It's *containing* the viewer with linear force, except for that of the privileged, heterosexist subject, who is totally empowered here by that reified aesthetic. It's so *line*-logical." I gave a thoughtful nod. *For fuck's sake. Idiot.* And what was he doing wearing a leather biker jacket? He'd never ridden a motorcycle in his life, I was sure of that. And that pathetic attempt at a goatee. It looked like the initial sprout of an adolescent's pubic hair.

"That's, ah, an interesting perspective. Does anyone want to comment on that? No?" *Please?* I scanned the rows; no takers, all busy with avoidance strategies.

"Okay . . . um, so you're saying that the aesthetic of the opening credits somehow privileges the male gaze because of its linear nature. That's a bit general, Gary, so can you drill down a bit?" *Christ, please don't.* Before he could respond, the door to the room came unstuck with a loud scrape. A reverse baseball cap head popped in and sheepishly withdrew, an early student for the next class.

Gary's puckered mouth, framed by the pubic goatee, was set to pass gas. I made quick note of the time on the large clock on the wall, directly above him. Five minutes. Why not finish a bit early? My flow was gone, the class showing its restlessness now. And I relished cutting Gary off. I took small victories where I could.

"Okay, we'll stop here. Stay warm on this unusually cool day, and for those of you who still haven't, please post your response papers by this evening, okay? I won't mark them as late." I gathered my notes from the lectern and slipped them into a worn manila folder with a half-moon coffee stain in its center. I made my way for the door, ping-ponging between students with questions, concerns, and triggers.

I stared at the empty space on my wood-paneled office wall, adjacent to my desk. Should I hang another movie poster? I had a first-print German poster of *Goldfinger* in storage ("James Bond ist Wieder in Aktion!"). Maybe it would be too busy. My office was cluttered already, and I'd been meaning to straighten things out, remove the stacks of paper and books that hadn't been touched in months. Unkempt. But the thought was fatiguing. I noticed my fingernails. *I should cut them soon.* I picked up my iPhone and read one new text on the screen, Paul wanting to meet for lunch in the faculty dining room. I replied affirmatively. I looked out the window at students milling around like sheep on the green. Mostly looking at smartphones, walking in patterns, their shoulders stooped and chins tucked, as if their necks were too weak to carry the weight. Some hustled around a noisy group of chanters with signs yelling something indecipherable beyond the glass of the window, but the tone conveyed the message well enough: indignation, conviction, fear, and judgment. *Good for you*, I thought. *Fight the power, stop the oppression, end the transgressions against the world you think you're owed. Get it out of your systems before you graduate to the professional class, join the firms, become an alumni donor, and pave the way for your offspring's legacy admissions.*

Plodding among the sheep were the supposed shepherds: professors with awkward marionette bodies transporting heads to classes or to department meetings where nothing would be resolved but frivolous battles would be fought, or perhaps to institutes and centers mounting vanity projects. I despised them, the arrogant entitlement, the sandbox hierarchies, the blindness to their ineptitude beyond their narrow, dissertation-defined lanes. I know—don't bother calling me a hypocrite: I was one of them. When properly motivated, I was a conspiring Brahmin in the caste, performing my rituals and sticking to the plan. I placed my peer-reviewed articles on the altar, did my departmental duties, gave my lectures, puckered up for the right asses, and completed my final induction into the tenure fold with the requisite overly narrow University Press book (*Giving Credit: American Film Credits and the Aesthetics of Preemption, 1945-1970*). How did I get here? Abbie, of course. I was, after all, a spousal hire, she being the real prize. I just came with the package (and thus avoided an exile offer in Nebraska). But that was fine—people liked me!

I first met her at the new-student meet-and-greet, recently admitted PhD students mingling with faculty and current students, compensating for nerves with peacocking intellects and ingratiating conversation. There she was: Abbie Stein holding court. One year in, she was already higher education royalty in lineage at the University. Two generations of academics preceded her there, both in medicine, both uniformly successful. "Pioneers in their fields" was a phrase I heard a lot, like it was an official title. But they were emperors, running research fiefdoms for the University, rich in grant cash and independent in authority. I was not a pioneer in my field. I had not been a star in my doctoral program, not like Abbie. The path on which I stumbled to graduate studies was not a linear one. In fact, each step of the way carried a sense of mishap, as if I had ended up lost and wandering in a large and imposing academic building, looking for the exit, but instead found myself stumbling into a classroom full of people who seemed to expect my arrival, had been patiently waiting to shout "surprise!" with perfunctory cheer. I would join the room, accept with resignation the pats and welcomes, pretend it was all my planned destination.

After all, it wasn't all totally unfitting; I'd been an excellent student in my western Pennsylvania high school, taking honors classes. Okay, it wasn't Andover, but even so, I did well. I suppose I got that from my Polish-American mother, who taught social studies in the town's elementary school. She quickly saw my aptitude and worked hard to nurture it. My father, of Irish-German descent, was a union electrician and viewed me with both pride and suspicion. I even served as editor of the school's literary magazine, *Book Bears,* named for the school mascot. "Hey, book bear!" my brothers would yell, leading to inevitable brawling and laughter (a high school wrestler, I usually bested them, joining in the howls).

A late arrival to the meet-and-greet, sipping from a plastic cup of sour California wine, I broke away from a stultifying conversation with a bad-breathed Victorian scholar and circled the outer perimeter of the cluster around Abbie. Her long black hair was perched back in a stylish clip. She was tall—just shy of six feet—and both willowy and athletic, half sitting on the arm of a chair, ready to spring up. She has a brown mole next to her right eyebrow. I thought it added an attractive fault to an otherwise symmetrical face—equine, Middle European, confident. She was striking, both in appearance and voice, which was rich and mellifluous. Her simple white blouse and chocolate pants were casually expensive.

"That's brilliant! You must be excited to work with Professor Weinrich. And how about you? What are you going to focus on?" She was interviewing the group around her, the host of her own talk show, and they were smitten. I grinned, still on the periphery and enjoying the spectacle. As she talked, her eyes would alight on me, very briefly and in sync with the rhythms of her sentences.

This went on for several minutes. I held my post, a silent, grinning sentinel, until she finally landed on me, turned fully and said in that resonant voice, "Welcome!"

"Hi."

"We were just talking about our areas; let me guess . . . Modernist?"

"American lit, mostly. Twentieth century, lit and film, actually." I suppose I was still grinning, by the way her eyebrows shot up. The rest of the group silently watched, heads at a tennis match.

"Film!"

"Yes." A pause. "I like to watch."

Uncomfortable silence. No one ever got the reference to my favorite film, *Being There*. Her slight smile dropped suddenly; she looked at me as if I were the small print of an instruction manual; and then, just as quickly, she matched my grin, then bark-laughed, tilted her head to the side, and came down from her perch.

Walking toward me, she said: "This wine is terrible. Do you want some more? Oh, look—there's Professor Bonner; trust me, she's as frightening as she looks. Come! Let's get some wine. What's your name? I'm Abbie. Oh, good—there's some cheese left. I'm starving! You're not from here, are you?" By evening, we were a couple.

"There's the Tickler with his new victim." I looked up from my soup. Paul did a subtle head nod to his left, to a deuce top against the wall of the dining room.

"Run to the exit now!" he stage-whispered. Paul Vartan was the closest thing I had to a friend and ally (friendships had never been a top priority for me). Two decades older, he'd introduced himself at my new-faculty orientation, where he'd given a humorous, even cynical, welcome. As he spoke, he caught the conspiratorial gleam in my eye and the suppressed smile and knew he had me hooked as an apprentice to friendship. He was one of the powerful University dons, so I was lucky to have his patronage. Old-school gay, sharp-tongued and stylish, he was fast to friends, a cutting opponent toward adversaries, never forgetting a slight or worse—an Armenian gypsy with a blood feud, for whom revenge was a duty. Paul also had the institutional memory of an elephant and knew where all the bodies were buried on campus.

I played along with Paul's theatrical gestures and looked past him to the esteemed Mark Pettersen, professor of early modern European history, author of many books I had not read, his blunt, chubby frame leaning forward on elbows as he spoke in secretive tones to a twenty-something graduate student. The Tickler, so called because of the many rumors about his proclivity to tickle his grad assistants. Despite the student's efforts to put on her best game face, she looked like a cornered lemur. I had a momentary, sharp urge to intervene and rescue, but you've probably discerned I'm not that kind of protagonist, and the moment quickly passed. Pettersen continued to mumble at her, licking his thin, pale lips in between bites of his sandwich. Something white and viscous was on his chin and it made me queasy. I looked away, put my spoon down and scanned the dining room. Mumbled conversations, some solitary diners; a few disheveled adjuncts hoping the brilliant light of the tenured would shine a miracle their way; a line of faculty at the dessert table, some gleamy eyed, others resigned to paunchy swells. The white tablecloths, large-windowed views, silverware, and cushioned seats couldn't disguise the room's true identity as a cafeteria.

"So, things patched up with Abbie?"

Here we go.

"Well, we didn't really need to patch anything. She's still on me, if that's what you mean. And I don't blame her. I just think her expectations have to be more grounded. I'm not her. I just don't care about the game as much—or I know I can't really compete in it the way she'd like me to. I don't know."

"Well, you haven't exactly been Johnny Lively lately," Paul said. "I don't know why; things are going well for you! You don't have to go out and win a Nobel. I don't think anyone's saying that." He looked at me with a mix of concern and expectation, trying to mask it with a casual lightness while fussing with his napkin. "I see your class is well enrolled—how is that going?"

"Seriously?"

"Well, come on! You have to get motivated for something. You just need to get your groove back." I'd never had a groove and didn't want one now. "Are you working on that article?"

"If by working you mean rewriting the same paragraph, every day, for the past two months, then yes."

"Give me a break. What am I going to do with you? Are you going to the conference with Abbie?"

"Again, seriously? Of course I'm not."

"It's Santa Monica—it will be pretty! You really need to stop this. You're becoming a big, fat bore. Well, not literally fat. Don't give me that hurt puppy look."

"Well, my pants are a little tighter—why do you think I'm having soup and salad for lunch? See, I'm not totally unmotivated. Proud of me? And no, I'm not going to troll around the conference carrying Abbie's books. She doesn't want me there anyway. I'm an unnecessary distraction."

I had hated academic conferences ever since my first one as a doctoral candidate, getting out there for the pending job market and giving a paper on movie credits. The three days of panels and meetings left me with a feeling akin to severe iron deficiency. At the end, a vortex of pinched faces and endless jargon-speak culminated in a reception and dance for the conference participants: gyrating, spastic academics undermining simple pop beats. Sweating, undulating, flailing with abandon, horrifying. I still bore emotional scars.

"Oh, boohoo. Who's going to change your diaper when she's gone?"

"Are you offering?"

"Please—at my age, I need to worry about my own diapers."

"I'm sure they're top brand and stylish. Okay, I have to shove off; want to walk out with me? The film program is sending over a replacement TA and I think she's supposed to drop by my office later. I should probably be there. You know, show basic interest."

"Oh, yes. Hopefully not a ward of the asylum like the last one."

My short-lived previous TA was a young man seemingly attempting to revive '90s goth. He was pale, nervous, and dressed in black or dark grey. He perspired regardless of temperature and was implacably consternated. After the first day of class, he went to the center of the campus green and began to scream, piercing and shrill, all while walking in a slow, clockwise circle. This went on for almost thirty minutes until befuddled public safety officers cut through the growing crowd of spectators and intervened. A dean of student affairs promptly sent a template wellness email to the student body. My former TA is currently on medical leave.

"Well, what do you expect from the MFA program? You have to document instability to be admitted. And how are the newlyweds?"

"Ah, Roger and his child bride."

Roger Croup was the chair of my department, and he also taught dramaturgy in the MFA program. The University has a policy against consensual student-faculty relationships, especially with undergraduates. Nonetheless, Roger had recently wed a newly graduated major from the department—two weeks after commencement. It was either an extremely fast romance, or their courtship had begun when she took his seminar.

They now showed up together at academic and social events where he introduced her with the flushed excitement of a boy who'd finally nabbed the present that eluded him for so many birthdays. She, saucer-eyed and talkative, was never unattached from his arm. The general counsel of our esteemed institution has the authority to grant faculty-student relationship exceptions—his extensive background in jurisprudence had equipped him with vast and nuanced insights into the ways of love—and the rumor was he had blessed Roger's. The thought of our diminutive, octogenarian general counsel reviewing and advising on various sexual and romantic practices was fodder for ridicule by many. (Paul, for example: "Should I ask Counsel what he thinks of my fellating technique? I hope it hasn't faltered through the years.") I suppose it was necessary. Attend the streets around campus, and one found not a few aging male professors pushing baby strollers around with exhausted resignation, an accepted concession to their marital trade-ins for much younger graduate students.

Paul and I strolled out into the briskness, each of us chuckling with the familiarity of an old couple and pointing out colleagues to be mocked. We parted after a while, he headed home, me back to my office. As I walked, I was weighed down by a sense of loneliness. The air chilled me, leaving me uneasy from fall's early arrival, intrusive and taunting.

I stared at the blank spot again, contemplating poster options. Loud exhales broke my trance and I turned from the wall. She stood in the office doorway, flushed and catching her breath. Had she taken the stairs up to the sixth floor? Unkempt and dramatically red hair sat asymmetrically atop her head, shaved on the right, rebelling on the left. Her expression, on an angular, freckled face almost severe in its lines, was concurrently stern, open, and comical, like a skeptical toddler in on a prank. Her eyes were a very dark brown. She wore blacks and purples, vintage clothing–store fashion, flowing and form-fitting on a medium frame. She stared at me as if in response to a challenge, one she would most certainly meet, then raised her eyebrows and said in a full but nasal baritone, "Professor Waite!"

I was thrown.

"Hello!" I replied. Why was I shouting? "How can I help you?"

I gestured to the seat across from my desk. She sat down, posture erect and still, her expression now disquietingly blank.

"I'm your TA," she announced.

Chapter Two

"Great! Welcome; glad to have your help." I thought it odd she'd announce herself as my TA with such authority, as if I'd had no final say (admittedly, I would have said yes to anyone with a pulse, but that's beside the point).

"All right, then. I'm Stacy, I should have mentioned—Stacy Mann."

She thrust out her arm, straight and centered, like she was aiming a gun at my chest. I couldn't possibly reach her over the desk—I was clearly too far away—so I thought it an odd gesture, but she held it there, expression still neutral but, under the surface, sizing me up. I got out of my chair awkwardly and came around the desk and she rose, her arm stiff and unmoving. I clasped her hand and the stiffness dropped and her arm became fluid, the handshake more of an undulation, an assortment of bracelets clinking out a brief melody. I was a beat behind the sudden kinetic change, like I was failing at a dance I'd been expected to learn.

She released my hand and sat down. As I returned to my desk, she said, "I promise not to scream."

"What?"

"We all heard about John, obviously." My institutionalized former TA. "We all saw that coming," she said. "He was pretty tightly wrapped. It's a stressful program, not for the weak. He was getting grief for his film thesis—we all do to some degree—but he was a rather delicate boy." She had the slightest of smiles.

She spoke about him as if he were dead, which, in a manner, I suppose he was. I settled back in my chair, trying to look relaxed, but the room felt crowded and the air heavy.

"Tell me about yourself. What have you been working on?" I said, flailing for something to say.

She now had a tilted smirk as if I'd said something amusing and looked to my right, past me. She continued looking at that spot as she talked, as if she were addressing a third person in the room sitting silently behind me. I stifled the urge to turn around and see who it was.

"I'm from Akron, originally—came here quite a while ago, though. Made my escape at nineteen and got a job as a photographer's assistant. I had no idea it would lead to a calling. It was just a job—wait!" she suddenly snapped. I jumped at the sound of my name. "Is that a *Casablanca* original? It is, isn't it! Holy shit!" There was a third person after all. I turned around and looked at Bogart on the poster. His world-weary face let me know life was all a fixed game—relax, have a belt, calm down. I exhaled and felt the tightness in my chest ease.

She got up briskly and skipped over, clapped her hands together, then leaned into the framed poster, putting her hand on the back of my chair. I could feel the heat from her body; she smelled of coffee and soap. I rotated my chair around and pointed to a faded autograph on the poster. "That's Sydney Greenstreet," I said, trying to blanket my pride.

"Bill Gold left out the gun in Bogart's hand on the first draft of the poster. Can you believe that? It would've changed the whole feel, taken out any menace or hint of violence."

I smiled with pleasant surprise. "You know Bill Gold's work? I'm impressed; not a lot of people bother with that stuff. What's your favorite Gold movie poster? Is this it?"

"*The Exorcist*, of course!" she said tartly, a hint of the pedantic. "I don't know. Perhaps others—they're all so good."

She sauntered back to her chair, looking around my cramped office, scanning the other posters, pausing at some with a nod, passing by others. The stone paperweight on my desk caught her eye. She picked it up. It was heavier than she expected and she cupped it in both hands, reading the chiseled inscription.

"'Oliver'?"

"Yes, that's my Oliver Stone," I said, humiliated by how stupid that sounded.

"Stop! That's insane—I want one. You should get a Sharon." She set it back down on my desk and returned to the chair. "So," she said. "I've never TA'd before, but I think I'll get the gist. Do you have anything for me?"

"Not really—the truth is, I could probably get by without a TA, but I know it's money for grad students. Trust me, I remember those days." I immediately regretted that. It sounded trite and condescending. "Just come to the next class. In the meantime, I'll add you to my course site so you can see what their upcoming assignments are. They have a short response paper due this week. We'll get coffee after class and I can catch you up," I added, impulsively.

"Okay, sure." Expression neutral again. "See you then." She got up to exit, smoothed her top and rolled her wrists, then looked at me, smiling: "Deliverance." She turned and walked out, calling back down the hall: "Bye!"

Deliverance.

Deliverance. Of course, the movie. She was referring to Gold's poster. I'd spent a few minutes after her departure pondering her cryptic meaning, casting the word as an elusive, almost mystical, sign. *No hidden message, idiot.* I was disappointed but quickly shut that down. I didn't want to admit that I enjoyed the idea that a secret meaning had been passing between us, nor my embarrassment at missing the obvious. I looked out the window at dusk settling in; another day folding away. They had all blurred into each other lately, but today felt different, marked like a placeholder in a book by an obtuse author, or perhaps simply a bad one. My phone vibrated and I welcomed the distraction: Abbie calling.

"Hi, hon—are you still on campus?" I said.

"Of course. I just got back to my office. I am so incredibly frustrated right now." She didn't have to tell me why; I knew what was coming. Abbie, appointed to more committees and task forces than sanely human, was chairing a faculty senate subcommittee of a committee (or a taskforce?), looking, broadly, at faculty diversity hires over the last decade, and she, more specifically, at gender ratios. "Meet me out front? We need to pick up some things before heading home," she said. I heard a muffled voice in the background.

"Is Terry fixing your coffee the way you like it?" Terry Rockford was her graduate assistant. Working with Abbie could make academic careers, so it was a coveted role. Terry, a dead ringer for a Ken doll, showed his unctuous gratitude with every breath and flash of his very white and large teeth. I was certain he'd come by and clean our bathroom, if asked, so I'd repeatedly prompted Abbie to ask.

"Oh, shut up with that—Terry? Yes, leave it there, thanks. So, ten minutes? Don't get lost on your computer watching movie trailers and make me wait. I don't have enough on, and the temperature dropped."

"Come on—that happened once." It had happened occasionally.

"No, Terry, that can stay." *Roll over, Terry; give me your paw, Terry.* "You know it's more than once. I'm not even going to ask if you wrote anything today."

"I think I have an extra scarf around here," I dodged. "Want me to bring it?"

"Yes! If you can find anything in that office."

"Maybe Terry can come by, straighten up?"

She sighed into the phone.

"Ten minutes."

I placed my iPhone down. Ten minutes was enough time to look up the *Deliverance* poster, which I only vaguely recalled. I entered a search on my desktop and it came up on the screen. I remembered now, one of Gold's stranger works: a huge single eyeball, a canoe with Jon Voight up front, rowing out of its center. I knew there was an alternative, less trippy, one, and I looked it up too: hands emerging from (or possibly descending into) the waters of the river, clinging to a rifle. Which one was she referring to? I made a mental note to ask. I thought either was an odd choice for a favorite Bill Gold movie poster. I felt disappointed.

"You need to cut your nails."

I rolled over to Abbie's side of the bed where she lay naked on her stomach. In the cusp of her lower back, little drops of sweat had settled. After the brisk two-block walk home, we'd bypassed dinner and had vigorous sex, an exorcism expelling the tension and anger pent up from her day. I had trouble keeping up and tried to mask my labored breathing, but I had to pause at times and gulp deep, wheezy breaths. She was a distance athlete, and I was out of shape—still residually strong from my wrestling days, but now better suited to hand water to the passing runners. I'd been ready to throw in the towel when she got on top to finish; the bed felt deliciously inviting under me. Nonetheless, I felt proud of my relative stamina.

I sat up and mimicked a clawing gesture. "This isn't a dream! This is actually happening!" I said, doing my best shocked Mia Farrow.

"What?" she said, distracted and distant.

"*Rosemary's Baby*. Come on, you know that scene. John Cassavetes, 'I need to cut my nails.' Satan's scratch marks." I ran my finger down her lower back and traced lines with her sweat.

"Not now with the movie trivia." She turned around and sat up. My hand slid off as her long torso stretched upward like a giraffe's neck. She was waiting for me to ask.

"So, what happened at the meeting?"

"Do you know that Malley had the nerve to claim progress? Progress being: we had an increase in the diversity of our applicant pool. But, of course, we hired only a tiny fraction of them." Malley was the provost's lapdog and point person on the task force, always ready to execute his derived power, which he did with collegial cheer.

"Are you surprised? I've said it how many times before: this is always the outcome on these things." I immediately regretting saying it, knowing I sounded more judgmental than I had intended.

Before I could retreat, she said, "No. I'm not surprised, obviously. Do you think I don't know this? I'm doing it because I want to hold them to the fire. I don't expect the administration to suddenly become enlightened to the fact that their so-called diversity initiatives are cynical window dressing. I could do nothing, I suppose. You'd advise that approach, I assume, since you've mastered it."

"Oh, come on, you know I'm not saying that—"

"Oh no?"

"It's just that I see how much stress it causes you, and I worry. It's not good for you. I'm sorry; I didn't mean to snap." I leaned over and kissed her shoulder. She was still for a while. Then I sensed the tension ease; she reached over and I leaned further in, kissed the point of her elbow.

"I know," she said.

"Are you hungry? Do you want me to dig up stuff? I'll heat it up for us."

"In a while; you go ahead," she said, leaning over to the nightstand where her laptop charged. "I have to reply to some of these emails from earlier. There's still some of the salmon from the weekend."

I knew that meant a half an hour, at least, so I kissed her again, she squeezed my arm, and I rolled out of my side of the bed. I pulled on shorts and a T-shirt, then went to the kitchen and opened the refrigerator, my bare feet cold on the tiled floor. In the back, behind the fish and partially covered with wrap, the remains of a layer cake from the previous weekend's social dinner. I maneuvered it out and cut myself a healthy piece, justifying my treat with the day's small lunch and evening's strenuous workout. This rationale didn't stop me from eating it quickly and silently, occasionally darting glances like a deer at a stream. In case Abbie broke from her laptop and approached, I was near the trash and ready to make a fast move. *I should have taken out the fish, left it on the counter as cover*, I thought, but I didn't get up, enjoying the cake too much to break off.

I licked the plate before putting it in the sink and went to the hall to grab my iPad and log into my course site. I was already behind on reviewing the current essay assignment, a short "reaction paper" on *Psycho*. I'd been assigning more of these short essays, not because of their pedagogical value (I'm sure it may exist), but because I could skim them. I hated reading student papers, especially the final essay, which required that I actually read them closely. Yes, a few were engaging, sparing me some pain, but most were tedious, obvious points dressed up with jargon and portentous syntax. I only reviewed them with precision from the fear that the students were onto me, that one would insert a trap sentence in the middle ("Professor Waite, are you reading this or smoking dope?") and my fraudulent engagement in teaching would finally get exposed, the scam over.

I added Stacy to the course site, giving her access permissions. After doing so, I smiled, thinking about her burst of excitement in my office, jumping up to my *Casablanca* poster. Perhaps I could ask her to review the essays. Was it too late? They were short, and it would be a good way to play catch-up and get a sense of the class. *It's still early*, I thought. *I'll email her now and give her the option, but no pressure if time doesn't allow.* I then thought about my misreading of her *Deliverance* comment. Why did I fixate so much on that? She was just making polite conversation. I was being ridiculous. Of course it was too late to ask her about the essays; she'd feel obliged as my new TA. Even though I was presenting it as optional, she wouldn't see it that way.

The cake was settling heavily in my stomach and I regretted eating it so fast. I set down my iPad and decided I would read the essays tomorrow. I shuffled into the living room, sank into the couch, and turned on the TV, flipping around until I landed on an old Western. I put my feet up on the coffee table, finding solace in the black-and-white images and the patter of rifle fire.

Chapter Three

Stacy exhaled a sweet-smelling vaporous cloud between jagged intakes of breath, clutching her e-cigarette with her left hand and wiping the runny mascara off her cheeks with her right. Her eyes were very bloodshot and still moist, but the worst seemed over. Students walked past us, some pausing briefly, others keeping their glances down as they scurried past. A few from class remained standing at a distance, voyeurism masquerading as concern. One of them was Gary Fallis. Stacy looked over at a young man who had stopped briefly to watch. He said something under his breath to his friend, who smiled.

"What the fuck are you looking at? Assholes!" Stacy said, punching her words. She gave them a feral look. They both assessed a response, saw the look on her face, and quickly moved on. I desperately wanted to join them. *Vanilla*, I thought, as more exhaled mist washed over my face.

It was Wednesday morning, and I'd been waiting outside of the lecture hall as students trickled in. I was expecting Stacy, who I'd emailed that morning. We'd agreed to meet a few minutes before the start of class. I held post by the door until it was a few minutes past, then walked up to the lectern. The students had mostly settled in, and I made small talk with a few in the front, keeping an eye on the door. Where the hell was she? I was surprised by my irritation with her for being late.

"So, I enjoyed your essays, some good insights!" I lied. I hadn't read them yet. "I'll post comments later this evening. Remember, you can always build on them as possible topics for the final essays." A hand shot up from a young man I'd dubbed the Simpleton, for his persistently stupid questions.

"You mean we can take one of the response papers and expand it into the final essay?"

"Yes, of course. If you find you want to explore one of them more deeply, definitely do so—I encourage you to."

"Do we have to choose our topic from one of the response essays?"

Unbelievable.

"Not at all—you're free to choose outside of them. Just remember, though, I want all of you to let me know your final topics beforehand so I can give you my thoughts, okay?"

The Simpleton raised his hand again; I pretended not to see it. I looked to the back of the room. Stacy was sitting there; when had she come in? Her head was slightly down and her arms were crossed. Gary Fallis was next to her, whispering and leaning in. She remained still and didn't acknowledge him. Was he bothering her? Should I intervene somehow? He stopped whispering to her and settled back into his seat, glancing over briefly. Stacy looked up and black lines streaked her face. Mascara? Was she crying? Her face was splotchy with red, only a bit fainter than her hair, and she was staring into her phone. Bad news? Something tragic? I had a fleeting impulse to excuse the class from the room.

We'd agreed I would introduce her to the class as the new TA, but I didn't know if I should proceed. While fumbling through some course generalities and fielding more questions about essays, deadlines, and grading, I made several attempts to catch her eye. Finally, she looked at me and I gave a quick shrug and raised my eyebrows. Yes? No? Her face gave away nothing. I was flying solo with this decision.

"Okay, before we dive in I want to quickly introduce you to our new TA, Stacy Mann, from the MFA film program. Stacy brings a lot of knowledge to the table and I'm sure she'll be extremely helpful as you home in on upcoming essay topics. Stacy?"

Heads turned to the back. Stacy sat composed, her face still somewhat blotchy but the mascara smoothed away. She gave a broad wave and said in a perfunctory but strong voice, "Hello. Looking forward to helping."

Heads returned to the front. All appeared totally normal, with no indications that any drama, big or small, had played out. She looked at me with that disconcertingly neutral expression of hers. I shuffled some papers on the lectern and began speaking about Norman Bates's passion for taxidermy.

I looked up at the wall clock; five minutes to go. I was anxious to end class and speak with Stacy, who had remained still throughout my lecture, almost catatonically so. Just as I was about to close out, I heard a loud humming moan, followed by what I can only describe as someone trying to sound off an *F* while inhaling.

"Fah-fah-fah!" Stacy punctuated each attempt with a head jerk, her iPhone clutched in both hands. Gary, still on her left, looked at her, then me, blanched and panicked.

"Faaaaah!" She bolted from her chair, grabbed her olive-green backpack, and was out the door, which she opened with a loud scrape, leaving it ajar.

The students whispered to each other, some looking concerned, others snickering, a few imitating the sounds she made. The Simpleton raised his hand and I ignored him.

"Okay, we'll pick up on Monday. Um—all right." I grabbed my folder and made for the door quickly. No students tried to intercept me; they were busily engaged in expressions of concern, gossip, ridicule. I noted that Gary was still in the back row, looking arrested. When I got out into the hallway, I caught a brief glimpse of Stacy going down the stairwell to the right.

"Stacy," I said, not loud enough to be heard. I clipped down the hall to try to catch up. *What am I doing? Let her go*, I thought. *Deal with it later; she'll reach out if she wants to.* But my legs kept going, and I went down the marble stairs with increasing speed, weaving around plodding students.

I pushed through the double doors leading to the lobby. I could see her through the ancient, beveled windows of the building's entrance. As I approached the door, the distorted view created a wavy effect that split her image in two: one tapered, the other wide. The distorted Stacy was holding an ominous black stick up to her mouth, and only when a cloud of vapor materialized as I exited the building and approached her did I realize it was an e-cigarette.

"Suh . . . sorry," she said.

"Are you okay?" I said. She paused, then looked at me with studied patience, sucking another drag and exhaling.

"Not really, but I'll be fine. Just the shock of it. My lover just cut me off in a harsh way, like I don't fucking exist, fucking bitch. I should have handled it better. It just threw me."

"Oh, I'm sorry! That must be hard," I said. *What an empty platitude. This is awkward. Get me out of here.*

She starting sobbing again, her temporary composure breaking. She moved into me quickly and, before I could react, hugged me closely and buried her face into my shoulder. I felt the damp heat of her face through my jacket and the eyes of spectators on my back.

⌁

"Anyway, that's how I ended up selecting the University's MFA program as my top choice."

We were sitting at a small round table that wobbled, near the exit of one of the campus's crowded coffee bars. The caffeine had enlivened her, and her spirits were up. She was animated and talkative, as if all that had preceded were inconsequential, forgotten. I was gorging on a cherry pastry with my coffee. The whole episode had left me frayed. The adrenal peak over, I needed a sugar fix.

"Slow down there! It's been awhile since I've performed the Heimlich," she said, and laughed. I put the pastry down, then picked it back up. "And Professor Creep—that's what I call Professor Croup, by the way—seemed to like my admissions loop, which I filmed in a warehouse in Berlin during an ayahuasca ceremony. He said the faculty admissions committee found it meta-performative, Warhol school—which, frankly, is not at all what I was going for, but whatever, it got me in the program."

"I'd like to see it; sounds interesting," I said. A group of hallucinating people in a warehouse sounded incredibly uninteresting, but what the hell; Professor Creep liked it. Very briefly, she gave a shy smile, and I realized she was flattered by my offer.

"So . . . anyway," she said, "sorry again about the emotional outburst. I hope I didn't frighten the precious undergraduates. I know how delicate they can be. We need to keep them safe."

This was unexpected and it prompted a smile. "I'm sure they'll be okay—a few triggered students will be fine. Maybe it will wake them up a bit." I had a sudden image of Nancy Butler, stern and maternal, the dean of Student Wellness and Inclusion, who'd run a training seminar for faculty chairs and directors, schooling us on student safety and wellness. I half expected her to appear and chastise me in her constrained voice, her outrage against the inhumanity of it all humming beneath the surface.

I changed the subject: "You're doing okay? Sounds like it was very sudden. Were you two seeing each other long?" Why was I asking this? *Switch back to her film studies.*

"Well, several months now. I met her through Gary. He and I'd been hooking up for a while, but that was just fun, nothing serious. And he's too young for me—he's just a boy!"

"Oh, so . . . Gary."

"He's okay. Yes, he's a pretentious prick, but it's his age. He is actually quite smart—he just thinks he has to play the role of intellectual. He's wearing it like a costume. And like most overconfident, elite freshmen his age, he's totally lacking in self-awareness, has no idea how he comes off." She looked at me and smiled. "I can tell from your expression that he irritates you. You know, he's probably trying to impress you. He's probably intimidated by you."

"I doubt that very much," I said.

"I don't," she said, examining me.

She swirled the paper cup and tilted her head back, downing the last foam of her latte. The bracelets on her arm tingled down toward her elbow, exposing two vertical red scar lines on the inside of her wrist. She saw me glancing at them and dropped her arm down on the table, staring at me with that now-familiar expression of challenge, those dark eyes locked. I averted my gaze to my iPhone, fumbled with its placement on the table.

"So, which one is your favorite—the canoe coming out of the eye or the creepy hands in the water?"

She gave me a perplexed look: "What do you mean? I don't understand."

"*Deliverance*. You said it was your favorite Gold," I said.

"No, I didn't. *The Exorcist*. I don't recall his *Deliverance* work, though I saw the movie, of course. First time I realized Burt Reynolds could actually act." She gave me a stare and smiled: "Oh, ha! I didn't mean the movie, silly. I meant being your TA. It's a deliverance."

"I—oh, I misunderstood. Okay. Um, from what?"

"What?"

"What are you being delivered from?" I asked. I was getting very uncomfortable but couldn't move away from it, as if in a tunnel that I desperately wanted to exit but felt compelled to see where it led.

"Boredom. And Pat, apparently—the girl that dumped me. What else? I guess we'll see." She dug into her jacket pocket and pulled out her e-cigarette. "I need a fix."

We got up from the table and worked our way through the narrow spaces of the crowded coffee bar. Outside, she inhaled deeply and released a sweet vanilla mist.

"I read the essays last night, by the way, after you added me to the site," she said. "I made comments on them. Do you want to see them? Or I could just send them to the class."

"Really? Yes, sure—go ahead and do that. Great!"

She paused, then reached out her hand: "Give me your phone."

"What? Oh, okay. Here," I said.

She handed it back: "Could you unlock it, please?"

I did. She took it back, tapped the screen and typed, tapped again and a ringtone went off in her jacket. She reached in the pocket and it stopped; then she handed the phone back to me.

"I've got your number. Mine's in your phone."

She inhaled and exhaled again, waved the cloud away, then waved at me and turned to walk away. I turned as well and walked in the opposite direction, not to any particular destination. The day's air was clear and warm, and I realized I was perspiring under my sport coat. I took it off and slung it over my shoulder. The sun felt refreshing on my face, and it thawed the clenched knot in my stomach. I felt, alternately and paradoxically, light and heavy, breezy and dense. I found my way back to the safety of my office.

Chapter Four

"Professor Waite, this is Pamela Ramirez-Jones from the Office of Equal Opportunity and Affirmative Action. Do you have a few minutes to chat?"

"Hello," I said. "Of course." My voice sounded hoarse and unfamiliar. I'd been in my office for the last two hours, in a quasi-fugue state, staring at the blank spot on the wall again. I wasn't contemplating movie posters this time; my eyes had settled there because it was the quietest spot in the office.

"This isn't a formal outreach, but we did have a student reach out because she was triggered by your physical contact with another student and the attention it got—well, you're already aware of that, I'm sure, so—"

"I'm sorry," I cut in, "I don't know what you mean. What attention?"

"Oh! Apologies. I'd figured you'd seen it online, in the *Beak*," she said. The *Beak* was the *University Beacon*, the fraught, declamatory undergraduate student paper.

"Can you hang on a minute, please?" I brought up the site on my desktop. Headlines: the student government issued a statement supporting dedicated space for affinity groups; the football team lost again; an opinion piece decried the response time for students seeking counseling. And, under Campus Sightings, a humor column, a photo of me hugging Stacy with the caption "Compassionate or Awkward? Professor Waite goes above and beyond." My iPhone vibrated on my desk. Abbie calling. I let it go to voicemail. I looked back at the photo. Stacy's back was to the shot, and she was nestled into my torso. My arms encircled, but my hands were flat and stiff, like flippers, barely touching her. My eyes were squinty and my face had a compressed look. I didn't recognize myself.

"Professor Waite, are you still there?"

"Yes. I, uh—so you're calling because a student is upset? Because of this photo?" I looked at the page again and clicked the "comments" icon. The first one read, "What's with his face? I can't tell if he's about to cry or if he's trying to get off." Eight likes, fifty-four more comments posted, most mocking me. I closed the page. My phone buzzed again: a text from Paul.

"Yes, we are not taking any formal action at this time, and the student will remain anonymous since there hasn't been a formal complaint, but I did want to bring it to your attention since there was distress caused and, I'm assuming, others may also have been triggered by the contact. But really, I don't want you to be concerned, just aware and maybe sensitive to the situation."

"Okay, so . . . yes. Thanks for the heads-up. I will certainly be extra aware of—well, of the situation."

"That's great. I'll reach out if there are further developments on this matter."

My phone vibrated again. Abbie calling a second time. I knew I should pick up. Instead, I stared at the phone. The door to my office was ajar, and I got up and shut it. I looked around the office. The clutter felt reassuring instead of burdensome—no longer a task to attend to, but stacked buttresses against an intrusive outside element. As I returned to my seat, my phone vibrated. I picked it up to view a text from Stacy: a single smiley-face emoji. I waited for another text to appear, perhaps words of explanation, but none arrived. I looked at the yellow smiley face again. It stared back at me with the indifferent malevolence of a child.

"Who *is* this person?" It was later that day. Paul was sitting behind his ostentatious wood desk, Armenian folk art hanging behind him. My eyes followed the circular pattern of interlocking women in colorful dresses on a weave design.

"Hello," Paul said. "Are you joining us today?"

"She's my new TA," I said.

"Oh, well, that's wonderful! She couldn't have the decency to leave you out of her public breakdown? At least your first one didn't involve you. And you thought it was wise to grope her in public?" He fussed with items on his desk, swiping away imaginary crumbs. Paul manifested agitation with fidgety hands. The more active they were, the greater the agitation. At the moment they were tapping out a frenetic score on an imaginary piano.

"She hugged me. What was I supposed to do, throw her to the ground and run?"

I was growing weary of this third degree. When I had finally returned Abbie's calls, she chastised me for creating an embarrassing public spectacle, then asked drilling questions about Stacy: *Who is she? Why was she hugging you? Is she stable? Didn't you vet her before taking her on as TA?* Thankfully, Abbie was guest lecturing at an event downtown this evening, so I'd have time to regroup and prepare for the deeper interrogation that was surely coming.

"Look, this is all silly. She was upset over relationship stuff, that's all. I don't understand the panic here. So, she got upset and some idiot took a picture."

"What did Abbie say?" Paul said, lips tight and eyebrows furrowed.

"What does it matter? She's reacting like you. I'm sorry to have caused a campus scandal. Christ, I should never leave my office," I said, embarrassed by my glum tone. "She's actually a very interesting person and I happen to think she'll be a very good TA. This whole thing is dumb and will be forgotten in a matter of hours. You know people on this campus have collective ADHD; some other click-bait will suck them in soon, probably already has. Frankly, this whole thing has been unfair for her."

Paul glared at me.

"It has," I said. "A student can't be upset without it becoming a major item? It's ridiculous and she shouldn't have to be outed like that."

Paul continued to glare, then asked, "Is there something going on between you two?"

"What? I just met her two days ago! Why would you ask that?" I said more loudly than I had intended.

"Because you've been a stick-in-the-mud and sleepwalking for months, and now all of a sudden you're passionate about defending some emotionally unstable student you've hugged in public. You haven't been that invested in anything recently, but you seem to be with her." His hands paused flat on his desk. "Perhaps I should thank her," he added, sarcastically.

"Well, what can I say? I think this is one silly overreaction and I don't get it. It's not about me being invested in her—though, like I said, she seems smart and will be a good TA. She's simply a student who now works for me and was distressed. Stop the freaking presses. What the hell is wrong with this place? You realize this is probably one of the most unimportant events ever, right? And Abbie wonders why I don't engage in the University more. This pathetic institution really needs to get out of its bubble and check out reality from time to time."

My phone vibrated and I pulled it out of my front pocket. Stacy was calling. I hit decline and sent a quick text, letting her know I was in a meeting but would call shortly. I looked up and Paul was stone still.

"Was that her calling?" When I didn't answer, he gave me a smug look, as if I'd admitted guilt before his tribunal. The sudden and alarming urge to get up and bash his face ran through me like an electric charge. The current permeated the room with lightning speed and flowed from me to Paul. He shrank in his chair and his eyes expanded. The surprising threat of violence crackled in the air, hitting us both on an atavistic level, then dispersed just as quickly, melting into the floor. We both sat still, uncomfortable in the silence and unable to give voice to what had just transpired. A chemical trace of threat lingered, and I scattered it with a warm smile.

"Yes, I told her to call and check in. I need her to review essays," I lied. "We do have work to do. I'm not totally ignoring my class." He tried to cover his brief shock with a nod and tap on his desk. We sat in a prolonged silence. "By the way, I think I had a breakthrough on my essay. I had an idea that seems very viable, so I'm going to kick it around, try to develop it." It was another lie. I hoped to ease Paul and shift back to a semblance of normalcy.

"Oh, that's good!" he said with forced cheer, as eager as I was to move on from the discomfort.

Our conversation puttered around, landing on casual topics and campus gossip, until I got up to leave and Paul said, "I know this TA stuff is just a distraction. You know I'm just looking out for you, right?"

"Of course! And I always appreciate it." I patted his shoulder as we both made our way to his office door. "Lunch tomorrow?" I asked.

"Indeed. We'll see who's drooling by the dessert bar."

I walked out of Paul's building and headed for the path that led back to mine. I was still sorting out the bizarre turn of our conversation, bothered by the sudden appearance of that violent impulse, when my phone vibrated in my pocket. I took it out and answered Stacy's second call.

Before I could say hello, she blurted, "So, how long are you going to keep me waiting?"

Chapter Five

The slender park west of the campus was teeming with afternoon regulars: dog walkers corralling happy, agitated packs; bored Caribbean nannies and young au pairs with little children who were screaming and working off sugar snacks by assaulting playgrounds and themselves, some with abandon, some cautiously on the periphery; a few retired professors consigned to benches, hunched exiles viewing objects and events out of reach. Stacy and I walked back and forth along one of the low stone walls adjacent to a linear path. We'd go on for a few hundred yards at a moderate pace, turn back, repeat.

"I mean, that's it, though, isn't it? This totally inbred and precious culture. Who the fuck cares who is happy, upset, hugging, fucking—whatever! And this giant eye monitors everything, keeping everyone in line or they go to reprogramming. It's all very, like, Maoist. And everyone is walking on eggshells, afraid to blunder into anything that could result in the usual social media ostracization. It's like we're all bubble-wrapped. The University is fucked!" She grinned and looked at me askance. "Too dramatic?"

"No, actually," I said. "It's the same through and through—students, professors, administration." I sidestepped some feces and continued on.

"Do you know a TV show from the '60s called *The Prisoner*?" I asked.

"Of course, cult classic. Patrick McGoohan. It's, like, the most ridiculously '60s-style show ever, psychedelic and totally *groovy*," she said, pronouncing the word with an Austin Powers British drawl.

"Ha, yes. Well, as a kid I was always spooked by that big white balloon called Rover that would roll after anyone who tried to escape the Village—you know, the prison, that's what it was called it: the Village. You'd get smothered and absorbed by it and it would simply roll you back to the place, where everything seemed fine, but it was still a prison. You couldn't leave it. You were trapped. So, no bars, no shankings in the prison yard, but it all seemed worse because even though it was a seemingly nice enough place, you were damned there. No more outside world."

"In other words, the University. You know, you kind of look like him—McGoohan. I guess that makes you the Prisoner!"

"I don't know about that. But I do admit, it does feel like that. Don't get me wrong, I'm lucky to have a professorship, especially here. Not a lot of work out there teaching and writing about films. I guess I shouldn't complain."

"Bullshit," she said. "Of course you should. I have no interest in that path. I'm glad to be able to work on my film and study with some good people—and have access to the studio and equipment I need—but I would never want to be a part of this culture. Too constraining! And, of course, I don't belong anyway. With my background, I'm not a member of this club. I didn't even finish my BA until I was twenty-five, and I went part time. I only decided on an MFA program because they dominate the film world now."

"I don't know about that. Academe is sort of a haven for those who don't fit in elsewhere."

"Superficially, yes. But let's face it, it's a self-generating organism that loves replicating itself and hates change. What's really different about it over the last few centuries? So the students look different, women and minorities can attend, big fucking deal. Most of the ones at this place still come from the privileged classes; and how many are mediocre legacy admits? If your parents went here, you just need a pulse to get in—or you can just leave a bundle of cash with Admissions. That's the University's dirty little secret. Superficial change! Look around. Same lecture style, same conservative traditions, same stupid hierarchies and titles, those ridiculous medieval gowns at graduation. And tenure! What the hell is that? Seriously, what a dictatorship it creates. If you have tenure, you can practically murder someone and you won't be fired."

"I'm not sure you could go that far."

"Yeah, you'd probably be asked to quietly retire if you murdered someone. Maybe. Professors: all just a flock of birds, squawking about in a language only they speak."

"It does sound like that sometimes."

"A murder."

"What?"

"A murder of crows. I picked that up in a medieval lit class. Apparently, some monks used the word *murder* to mean a flock of crows."

She paused to look out past the stone wall, distant city traffic whooshing by beyond the trees. I stopped and looked too, but wanted to keep moving, like the cars. Technically, we were just pacing, but I felt like I was making progress on a journey and I didn't want to pause. I wanted to reach this destination, to see what was at the end of the road.

"You can ask about it. I know you're curious," she said.

"What do you mean?"

"My wrist. The scars."

"Oh. It's none of my business."

She turned to me abruptly. "I hate it when people say that! 'It's none of my business.' What that really means is, 'Don't make me uncomfortable by discussing your aberrant behavior.' Don't do that, Daniel. You should know better. I just gave you permission to ask. Don't hide from that."

I was taken aback by the direct confrontation in her words, the use of my first name, the underlying anger and judgment. But then she looked at me, her face that neutral mask she'd worn before, but now with a slight smile. I found it incredibly unnerving, and I thought back to the yellow smiley face. I struggled with the urge to ditch her, to hurdle the wall and hide among the trees, but I held my ground.

"I'm not afraid or uncomfortable," I lied; I was both. "I really didn't want to pry. It's my upbringing, respecting the privacy of others and all that. Tell me about it, if you want to."

"Well, sorry to disappoint, but it's the typical boring, fucked-up story. Such a cliché: sixteen with an abusive, alcoholic father and a passive mother, not fitting in and labeled as part of the freak crowd—which I was, no other option in Akron. I was also using too much, a lot of coke and weed, mostly, some Vicodin . . . and then when I got pregnant, I just wanted to check out. Looking back, I think that was my way of getting an abortion, getting rid of it. I was just sort of collateral!" she said in a cheery tone. "I was already doing some self-cutting, so it seemed like the logical method." She held up her wrist and shook her bracelets.

She reached into her bag and pulled out her phone. She read the screen, tapped away, and read it again.

"Gary. He's worried about me. That's kind of sweet, but he's also a bit of a stalker. I haven't quite been able to shake him off, the little pest." She scratched the shaved side of her head. "Come on, want to go further?"

We continued on.

"Just black, right?" she asked.

Hardiman Arms was an old, prewar building of red brick, sturdy and broad with a courtyard entrance. Like many of the large apartment houses around campus, it had been purchased by the University decades ago and converted into student housing. In Hardiman, it was predominantly graduate students, the old, grand apartments refitted with cheap walls to contain more heads per apartment. The ceilings were still high, though, creating an odd effect in the smallish rooms, like they were silos into which people were dropped. I looked around Stacy's apartment: an expensive-looking mahogany cabinet; found objects placed thoughtfully, including an old, dented stop sign; books neatly placed in two tallish bookshelves;

a small white corner desk with a laptop; two framed movie posters, one *Notorious*, the other *The Crying Game*. I was surprised by the apartment's tidiness. Everything in its place, and very clean. This was not at all what I'd expected. I didn't expect to be here at all. Stacy walked out of the galley kitchen with an antique-looking tray holding two porcelain cups.

"Thanks," I said. The blue-and-white cup looked silly and dainty in my hand. I took a sip and placed it on the side table. I looked out the smallish window off to the right, which faced an alley. A brick wall stared back. Muffled voices came from a neighboring apartment, but I couldn't tell if it was from above or an adjacent one. Late afternoon was eyeing the exit, and only then did I realize that a good amount of time had passed since we'd met up. The apartment was dim, and Stacy reached over and clicked on a small lamp with a beige cover. The whole apartment felt like a stage set, one totally incongruous with the person who lived in it. I had the tingling feeling a hidden viewing audience was watching.

What was I doing here? It seemed so natural to tag along, just an inconsequential stop on our peripatetic engagement, but as we walked into the building's courtyard, I saw the black orb of a security camera above the entrance. It looked at me like a shark's eye, predatory and indifferent. A few students were leaving as we entered, but they seemed uninterested in us. I thought, *Perhaps no one cares if I'm here. She is my TA, after all.* But now, sitting in the chair, taking another sip of coffee from the tiny cup, my overriding thought was *Extricate yourself soon and leave before evening sets in.*

"You look distracted," Stacy said.

"No, I'm fine. It's just been an interesting day. Again, I'm sorry about all that's happened. Are you feeling any better about Pat? The breakup?"

She waved me off. "It's stupid. I probably was just upset I didn't beat her to the punch. I was just reacting to the rejection." She took out a vaping device, different than the one I'd seen earlier, from the drawer of the table that held the lamp and took a hit. She exhaled, and the pungent smell of weed filled the room. She held it out to me.

"I really shouldn't. I haven't smoked weed in a long time and—"

"—and what. You have work to do tonight? No, you don't. I took care of it, remember? It's mild and, frankly, you look pretty constipated sitting over there," she said. She grinned. "But I don't want to get you in trouble with Professor Stein."

"Funny. Okay, one hit." Abbie was exactly who I had in mind. The day had been bizarre enough, and the thought of facing her questions later that night with heavy lids and bloodshot eyes only added to my dread. But it was still early enough, I supposed, and it was just a bit of weed. Perhaps it would do me some good, relax my mind. I took it from her, inhaled deeply, and expelled the mist. She looked at me with satisfaction while texting away on her phone. Not at all like the joints of my youth, which always scorched my lungs and led to coughing spasms, and laughter about the spasms. This was easy, smooth, just like breathing pleasantly warm air.

I took another hit.

Chapter Six

"This part is my favorite."

A close shot of a heaving back. An outline of a spine visible through a tight beige shirt, writhing like a snake. Retching sounds, then the splash of liquid. The shot pans over the back, lingers briefly on matted brown hair, and then focuses in on a spillage of vomit next to a red ash bucket. An undigested yellow-green pea floats in the middle of the spew, and the camera locks in on it. While the image made my stomach flutter, the aesthetics worked powerfully—the lighting and flow give the shot the feel of traversing a surreal landscape. Or maybe it was just the weed and the two beers.

We'd been discussing film for over an hour, and I was amazed by her knowledge of film history. She knew trivial details of movie favorites that I'd kept locked in my memory like a reference archive, and I was happy to unpack them. I was excited with nerdy joy when she carried on about the Freudian elements in *The Red House*, one of the best psychodramas of the '40s, with a brilliant performance by Edward G. Robinson. She knew all the scenes and some of my favorite lines, and we laughed at our poor attempts to mimic Robinson's iconic voice. It was when we turned to Kubrick that she'd led me over to the white corner desk to show her work.

"This is actually quite arresting. The camera work is excellent." I leaned over Stacy's shoulder while she sat and worked at her computer. We'd been watching various cuts for a while; I was getting tired of standing, and my eyes felt strained. She pushed back her chair and walked into the galley kitchen. I sat back down.

"Yeah, thanks! So far, I think it's going in the right direction. I think I have enough raw material, so the shooting is pretty much done." She walked out with two more Coronas and handed me one. I took it and placed it on the side table. My head was beginning to hurt, not helped by the loud bass thumping from the apartment next door, mixed with excited voices, laughter, some shrill hooting.

"That happens a lot here," she said, aiming a thumb at the wall. "I don't mind it. I just block it out when I'm working and usually pop over after. Want to go party with students, Daniel?" She gave me a mocking look, and I grinned.

"I think I'll pass," I said. "I doubt they'd want me skulking around. That'd be pretty awkward." I settled back in the chair. My mouth was uncomfortably dry and I took a sip of beer. Had the apartment gotten smaller? The walls felt closer and stifling. The pleasing buzz of the weed had begun to slide away, leaving me foggy, the first traces of paranoia playing at the edges. My limbs felt stiff and clumsy. Stacy sat on the rug and hugged her legs with her arms, as if performing a cannonball dive.

"Don't want to be seen with me in public?" she asked softly, her face serious and open. Before I could fumble out a response, she burst out in laughter and pointed at me. "Relax! I'm joking! I'm not going to drag you over to a party of students so they can gossip about us. We've given them enough with that fucking ridiculous photo today, don't you think?"

I smiled casually, trying to make light of it. But I was growing increasingly worried about my exit. I really didn't want to run into any students I knew—not here, not in my current state.

Stacy texted briefly and then stretched out on the rug. "So, what's it like being married to an academic superstar?" she said, staring up at the ceiling. "I mean, she even looks like a superstar. Is she taller than you? I read all four of her books, and they're not even in my field—plus, you know, I don't consider myself an academic—but her writing is so damn appealing. I really got into *The Female Clavicle*. Does she have normal conversations or does she, like, only utter profound insights? 'Daniel, I sense a paradigm shift in the urban aesthetic vis-à-vis pedestrian performativity. Pass the salt, please.' Ha—it's hard to imitate that musical richness in her voice."

The mockery in her tone, coupled with that disturbingly blank expression, jabbed me. And she did sound a bit like Abbie; it was unsettling. She grabbed a small, round pillow and placed it under her head, which tilted up from the floor at an extreme angle. It looked semi-detached. The skin on her face was translucent. Her eyes were bloodshot and her freckles stood out dramatically. Her hair was fiery, unkempt. She was Linda Blair in *The Exorcist*, sans the mauled face and Satan voice. I half expected her head to perform a 360-degree rotation. The back of my neck tingled. *That's silly*, I thought, and shook it off. I was definitely feeling worse, my pounding head syncing with the loud thump of the bass. It was all a depressing slide from earlier.

I'd enjoyed connecting with Stacy, walking with her on the outer perimeter of the campus, watching her film and discussing edits, diving into movies. I'd not been my usual laconic self; the strange energy of the day had driven me on and I needed to purge it, run it off. But it was more than that, I had to admit. I was excited to unload on the reviled University, for her to confirm my frustrations with the whole scene. She got it. Like me, she was an outsider to the pretentions and incestuous culture. And she saw the fraud of it all. She was like a clandestine visitor to the Village, arriving to confirm that I wasn't crazy, I wasn't delusional, offering me a brief sense of deliverance (no, the word wasn't lost on me).

Abbie, Paul, my colleagues—they all saw my complaints and resistance as an unfortunate manifestation of my scholarly doldrums, the untethered and, yes, lazy self-involvement of a privileged spousal hire. If I simply worked harder, got involved, wrote more, came to meetings. I was the issue and I didn't appreciate what I had. *Snap out of it and stop being so low-energy, embrace what you have, it's the envy of so many. You're tenured at the*

University, for Christ's sake, you snatched the golden ring! Stacy's welcomed complicity fueled my growing ire, egged me on. I finally had permission to speak out.

At the same time, being with Stacy felt like watching a split screen of two films with opposing narratives. She was an ally in one; she was a strange entity, watching me with clinical blankness, in the other. She was eccentric and quirky; she was watchful and judgmental. Was I a kindred spirit or a specimen? Which movie was real? Perhaps neither. Was she simply putting on an act for me? Maybe she was just having fun, entertained by my state, enjoying the pathetic spectacle of the whiny professor hanging out in her apartment, smoking weed and drinking beer. After all, I didn't really know her—anything about her, really. Just what she'd shared and my early impressions. And her oddness could be jolting. But I wanted to dismiss this as paranoia. *Look at her; look at how she acted today, the emotional outbreak.* The scars on her wrist were real. No, she was eccentric, even a bit off, but that must be real, too. I looked at her and she was texting again. She'd been doing so throughout the evening. Who was she texting? Gary? Was she sending him updates on me? Was that pretentious little weasel part of the plot?

"Oops, I think I hit a sore spot," she said.

"No, no—I'm just crashing from the day." I yawned to underscore my point and took another sip from the beer bottle.

"Bullshit! See, you're doing it again."

"Doing what again?" I tried to sound casually irritated, but it came out as startled.

She bolted upright. "What have we been doing here, Daniel? Don't keep opening and then shutting the door—and don't give me that perplexed look. I see right through it. You, my friend, are in crisis, and the only way through it is to stop pretending." She stood up and moved toward me. "Stop pretending with me!" she shouted, pounding out the last two words and jabbing me in the chest. "Being passively in denial is not going to help you. Besides, it's disrespectful."

I just stared at her. That goddamn word again. *Passive. Do something,*

Daniel—you're too passive. Write that article, get excited, go to meetings. I had the urge to scream but stifled it.

She stepped back a bit. "Stand up."

"Really? Okay—I probably should head out soon anyway . . . "

"Shut up. Come here." She looked at me with that familiar, irksome smirk. I lifted myself out of the chair and took a step forward. She considered me for a few moments, then shoved me hard. I fell back into the chair.

"What the hell?" I said. She smiled and said, "Stand up. Come on!" I let out a breathy sigh and stood again. She moved in to shove me and I held firm, but then she gave me a quick, sharp jab in my abdomen.

"Ow! What the hell?" The surprise of it made me laugh. "Don't make me hit back," I said, attempting to sound playful.

"That's the problem. You won't. I think you like the punishment." Her breathing was getting a bit heavy. Her nostrils flared.

"No, actually, I don't like punishment, thank you very—" She slapped me across the right cheek, hard enough for it to sting. I glared at her, my anger flaring. I started forward, then caught myself.

"Oh, ho—what do we have here?" she said. "Do I see some real anger? Finally, am I reaching you? Is there going to be some action from mild-mannered Professor Waite?" Her smile flashed small, white teeth: her eyes were wide with excitement. She began moving her weight from side to side, like a basketball player, her arms up in the ready position. I wanted to reach over with both hands and smother her irritating face.

"This is silly. I'm leaving. It's been an exhausting day and I think we both could wind down a bit." I started for the door.

"Wait! Don't go yet—I'm sorry!" she said. She grabbed my forearm as I walked past her and I paused. "I know I get a little intense, but I didn't mean to push you. I've done way too much fucked-up behavioral therapy and sometimes I can get confrontational, I know. But I meant well, I did! Please, stay a little longer. Please. I don't want us to end the evening on a bad note. I feel like I've ruined everything." The vulnerability in her expression stopped me, the look of hurt and dismay. I wanted to escape, but I suppressed the impulse when I saw tears welling up.

"Hey, it's okay." A tear ran down her cheek. "Really, I can get the same way. You're direct; that's not a bad thing, believe me. Your bluntness is actually refreshing—" With sudden speed, she jutted her face toward mine, baring her teeth as if to bite me; I recoiled, then she feinted low, stepped in, and struck me, harder than before—a full, open-handed right hook with her weight into it. She released a high-pitched, joyful scream that turned into a laugh while she ran to the other side of the room. She looked back over her shoulder briefly, snatched her phone off the floor and started texting maniacally.

I was across the room in a flash. I grabbed her from behind by her elbows and flung her arms to the left. The phone flew out of her hands and hit the wall. She bellowed, then pushed back into me, and my arms slid up into a rear choke hold, muscle memory from my youth taking over. Her bellow turned into a piercing, shrill scream that momentarily stiffened me. In a panic now, I squeezed my right arm into her neck, her trachea untouched in the crook of my elbow. I grasped my left bicep with my right hand, and my left pressed into the back of her neck. I continued to squeeze, lateral pressure cutting into both sides of her neck, muffling her cries. She flopped around, survival reflexes taking over as her breath was stifled. Her right leg kicked into the wall in front of us, the thump blending with the bass and loud voices on the other side. I pulled her back from the wall and applied more pressure.

Her flailing movements tapered off until she was loose and floppy in my arms. I brought her gently to the floor, where she lay still on her back. She had a flushed, peaceful expression on her face and beaded sweat on her nose. I waited over her, knowing from experience that she was moments away from regaining consciousness. I also knew that could be disorienting, could result in jolting alarm. It was all so detached, so clinical as I stared down at her. But I was suddenly and violently bludgeoned with the realization punching dread to my core: This was bad. This was very bad.

Her heavy eyelids fluttered open; she looked around, dazed. She still had a serene expression, and I thought I caught the beginning of a slight smile touching her lips, as if waking from a very pleasant nap. Then her eyes focused on me as I leaned over her. Her expression changed instantly to animal fear.

"Wait! Wait!" she panted, holding one hand turned up, as if making an offering.

"I'm so, so sorry—I really didn't mean for it to happen. I don't really know what happened. You were acting so wild, the noise, I panicked . . . "

"Wait, okay?" she said. "Just stay there, please?" She held her offering hand. I didn't know if she was blocking me or wanted a lift up. I stayed very still, groping for something to say, some explanation. She rolled to my left very quickly, her arm reaching for something. She yanked a nearby power cord out of a wall socket and her laptop flew off her desk. She whipped the cord at me and I held up my arms to block it, trying to snatch it away from her. She became entangled in it as she rolled further and up on her knees. She got her bearings and stood, then tugged the cord, and I tugged back. Realizing there was no helpful purpose in our tug-of-war, she released the cord and turned back to the wall, pounding it with her fists.

"Help me! Help!" she screamed.

"Wait!" I said. I had the cord in both hands, and I swooped it over her head and pulled her back from the wall. She reached up to lift it over her, and I closed in quickly and tightened the slack in my grip. She briefly pried at her neck, where the cord had settled tightly, and then reached her arms out, trying to touch the wall as if it were a finish line. I clamped down harder on the cord to keep her hands inches away from the wall, afraid to let go. She pulled and reached; I pulled and twisted. She let out a stifled, nasal hum as her arms waved, the bracelets clinking a broken melody. With surprising strength, she lurched forward again, almost reaching the wall. I nearly stumbled, and to regain my balance I pulled back violently. I heard a crunchy snap, like stepped-on branches, and she dropped like a heavy sack. I released my grip on the cord.

She was on her stomach, and I slowly rolled her over. She was perfectly still. Her wide eyes stared at me with surprise and indignation. The cord was still wrapped tightly around her neck. Her tongue protruded slightly from her mouth, teasing and comical. A swell of shouts and hooting suddenly rose up from next door, then subsided. My hands began to shake, and I had the sudden need to void my bowels. I ran to the small bathroom past the kitchen, just making it to the toilet. The splashing sound brought me back to her film clip, the arching back and green pea, and I whispered to myself: "Dead."

I could see her still feet from the open bathroom door. I sat there, stuck, unmoving except for my shaking hands. I stared at her feet. Why hadn't I noticed she wasn't wearing shoes? Her socks were powder blue. I sat and stared at them for several more minutes, then cleaned myself and flushed. I walked over to her, stood for several minutes like a frozen sentinel, then found my way to the chair and sat. I looked up at the framed poster of *Notorious*. Ingrid Bergman with a tea cup, looking both conspiratorial and frightened. I dug my phone out of my pocket. I went to my contacts list, scrolled down, and hit the call icon. On the fifth ring, she answered.

"Mom," I said.

Chapter Seven

"Hi, Danny! Is everything all right? It's not like you to call on a weeknight. Is Abbie okay?" she said in her two-tonal pitch of warmth and worry.

"Everything's fine. I just have some downtime and I thought I'd check in since I was too busy to call last weekend. How's Dad?" I stared down at Stacy's socks.

"Oh, fine. Asleep in his chair, as usual. Working too much, but I can't get him to slow down. He's doing much better. The Lipitor seems to be helping, but of course I can't get him to change his diet. Are you eating better? I imagine Abbie looks out for that. She tells me when you're not, you know. She's my partner in policing you!"

Mom worshipped Abbie; she viewed her as the pinnacle of female achievement (in education, no less—my mom's great love). Abbie was like a distant icon she'd never reached from her perch as an elementary school teacher. My marrying Abbie was pure affirmation for Mom: her son had found love with an aspirational version of herself. Abbie, no stranger to a fan base of young academics hoping to leech off her influence, was atypically moved by mom's clear adoration, which she embraced fully. The two of them could be a bit much.

I scanned up from Stacy's feet and saw that she had emptied her bladder, a wet outline just visible on her dark pants. A faint trace of steam rose from it.

"Danny? Hello?"

"Sorry—yes, I'm listening. I just got distracted," I said.

"Are you all right? You sound tired."

"Oh, a bit. It was a busy day, so—"

"Are you writing? Abbie told me you were working on something and I know how stressed you get when you are. Since you were a boy!"

"Mom. Do you ever see John Costello around? Does he still live in town?"

She paused, then said, "Oh, I don't know. Oh, Danny—why bring him up now? That was so long ago. Have you been thinking about it? Is that what's bothering you?" I wasn't fooling her with the tired routine. She had microsensors that sifted through every change in tone and pattern. And she would push, obliquely and with finesse.

"No, no. I saw someone with an eye patch today and it just reminded me, that's all," I lied. "I just got to wondering if he was still around."

"Well . . . " She paused again. "I suppose I may have seen him a while back. I'm sure he's doing fine." A silent pause. "I know I've said this a million times, but it wasn't your fault. You were kids and he shouldn't have kept pushing you. And he was a year older! I'm not saying I don't feel bad that it happened and that you both had to go through all of that, but it was an accident." The images came fast: the stick rammed into John's eye, the wet popping sound, the suspended moment of disbelief following by screaming, John running down the hill and away, the protruding stick swaying like a metronome.

"Oh, I know; I really hardly think about it. It was just that guy I saw, that's all, and I was curious. That was so long ago."

Her pause was an acknowledgement of my falsehood, but, departing from precedent, she didn't press me further. Perhaps she knew on some deep level that I couldn't go there. We talked a bit more, trivial banter, and ended with my usual promise to come visit when we could. I ended the call and closed my eyes. A stream of realizations circled my head like a flock of manic crows: *I am in my TA's apartment. She is dead. I killed her. I am surrounded by students. I was filmed entering the building. I strangled her. I'm coming off a buzz. I've been here for almost two hours. I have to do something. I have to get out. I have to call the police. Abby's going to kill me. I can't call the police. I have to do something. I can't tell Paul. I can't get caught. I should confess everything that's happened. I can explain all. It was an accident. I strangled her to death.*

I opened my eyes and she was still there. Of course. *It's not a dream, idiot.* I took out my phone. *I have to call 911*, I thought. *What else can I do?* I stared at the phone. *No, no, no—I have to fix this. I can't be found out.* I stood up from the chair, put my phone away, and shook myself.

I had to do something, but what? *Obviously, I can't just leave*, I thought, *but what am I supposed to do first? Think.* I looked around the room, then walked into the galley kitchen. A small, neat counter. A coffee maker, paper towels, another phone charger plugged into an outlet above the counter. To the left, a narrow window with a purplish shade, a step stool beneath it. *Window!* I scurried back into the living room: two windows. *I could have been seen!* No shades, just diaphanous curtains pulled to the sides. I sat back in the chair, looking around. I could see through the near window, as before. Just the wall looked back. *The light!* I got up and turned off the lamp, making the room darker, but not by much.

I slowly approached the second window, keeping a distance. No sightlines from this location. I closed in and looked out from a side angle: a window to another apartment down the alley, at a distance to my left. Darkness behind the white blinds. Not at all a good view into the apartment. *But could they have seen something earlier, somehow?* Perhaps they did, then closed their blinds out of fear. They could have heard her screams, then strained to look in. They could have called the police already—I had to get out now. They could show up any second.

No, no, no—I was panicking. The sightlines were too obscured. I looked again. *Did the blinds just move?* Yes! There, I spotted a fluttering motion. Someone was peeking at me. A small, ginger head protruded from the side of the blind and stared at me. It took several moments for me to process that it was a cat. We locked glances; in its expressive green eyes I read curiosity, then predatory complicity, and, finally, indifference. It became bored with me and retreated from the window, off to eat, nap, or chase string. I found myself grateful that it wasn't a guilt-sniffing dog, alerting the human gods with its barking diligence.

I walked past Stacy's body, not looking down, and stood at the entrance of the tiny bedroom and peered in. Just large enough for a queen bed, neatly made with a paisley duvet, and a narrow wardrobe unit, walnut brown and rather fancy with carved lattice woodwork along the back frame. Two stacked books with a small brass box on top. One window, a blackout shade pulled down. *No need to go in—leave everything undisturbed*, I thought. I passed the bathroom heading back to the living room, paused briefly to glance in, then quickly peeked behind the shower curtain, compelled by the irrational idea that someone was hiding there. All clear, just shampoo, conditioner, and a thick bar of black soap. Abbie had mentioned wanting to try that type. Was it West African soap? *Abbie.* I shuddered and looked at my watch. She was probably in the middle of her talk.

Back in the darkness of the living room, I stood and looked around, but no answers presented themselves. I walked over to Stacy and leaned down to view her more closely in the dark. Her eyes were still open. She was staring up at the ceiling like a surprised child. The thin, white cord around her neck looked like a simple fashion accessory. Both arms were at her sides, palms up. I examined her left arm and saw the scars on her wrist, unobscured by the bracelets, which were bunched together. Under closer scrutiny, the lines of both looked more prominent than before, when I had just stolen a glance. She'd really done a number there. I felt an overwhelming sadness at the thought of it and, oddly, a spasm of loneliness. My stomach churned again, but then settled. How had this happened? How did I get here? I shook off the speculation. This was no time to ruminate; I had to move, had to come up with a plan. The clock was ticking.

I picked up the laptop from the floor and placed it back on the corner desk. I couldn't plug it back in without removing the cord around her neck, and I didn't think I had the nerve to do that. I stopped; a thought came to me suddenly. *Suicide. She did this.* With her history, would that be so surprising? *But how? She strangled herself while I sat and watched, drinking beer?* To anyone who inquired, it would be known that I was in the building. But the camera would see me leaving, too. Who's to say I was present when she killed herself? I was there, then I wasn't. I tried to console her, then had to leave. I did what I could. I looked down at her again. This wouldn't work; she clearly looked like what she was: a strangling victim. My chest tightened as I contemplated that. What else could it be? Autoerotic asphyxiation? Wasn't that a thing? But no, that would, by implication, make my presence here a scandal. Abbie would strangle me. *Oh, hell*, I thought, and held my stomach.

As I examined her neck I was interrupted by an idea. *Perhaps . . . yes, it could work.* I walked into the kitchen and started going through the cabinets and drawers. Utensils, dishes, glasses, takeout menus—and I saw it, neatly rolled up. An extension cord. I pulled it out and also grabbed the phone charger cord on the counter. I dropped both in the middle of the floor and returned to the bedroom. The narrow spaces on each side of the bed were uncluttered. Only one outlet with a plug to the lamp on the bed stand. That wouldn't work. I went back into the living room and unfurled the extension cord, discovering that it was fairly long, perhaps nine feet. That could work. I wouldn't even need the phone cord from the kitchen.

I moved over to Stacy's body and squatted down. I knew I would have to remove the laptop cord and replace it with the extension cord. But could I do that without subverting the appearance of it all? I'd watched *CSI* a few times, enough to know I was already in amateur territory. There were probably screaming clues everywhere and my set-up would explode with blunders.

But that was TV. The police I'd encountered or seen in interviews didn't strike me as particularly bright or motivated. Didn't they just want to close cases? Wasn't that what it was really like? Incurious, average guys wanting to clock out, go home to dinner. And campus public safety wasn't a concern. Those guys were total incompetents. If it looked like a suicide by a student with a history of suicidal behavior, would they really scan for deeper clues? And suicide was so common now; how many hand-wringing committees and task forces had the University formed in the last few years in response to the growing cries about the stress culture, lack of wellness interventions, and student suicides? It seemed like there was one or two deaths every year, sometimes more. And what choice did I have? It was the best I could do. I had to get out of there.

I looked more closely at the cord around her neck, then gently rolled her over. She was heavy and floppy. I ignored the smell of urine as best I could. The cord was loose in the back but seemed to be holding tight in the front, as if glued to her skin. Probably wedged in due to the force of the pull. I'd have to peel it off; what else could I do? The extension cord was thicker, so maybe it would cover the initial indentation from the thinner laptop cord. I could try to fit it in and pull, get it to tuck in.

I collected the extension cord and rolled Stacy over once again. I pulled the laptop cord slowly from her neck. It caught a bit, and when I fully peeled it back, a red, indented line traced across her neck. I took one end of the extension cord and placed it on the red line. Then, with both hands on either side of her neck, leaving enough length to knot it off in the back, I pressed the cord in, gently compressing it with my fingertips. The skin on her neck was spongy and already turning shades of purple and blue from the bruising. I rolled her back over, carefully holding the cord in place along the front of her neck. I then tied the end of the cord off, making a firm and ugly knot. I rolled her back over and examined my work. Yes, it seemed to be right in place. This would work. I got up and carried the laptop cord over to the corner desk and plugged it back into the wall, connecting it to the computer. *Now, where to hang the body?*

Chapter Eight

*B*ody, I thought. *No longer a person. Stacy was here, and now she is not.* She evaporated, blew away like dust. No, she didn't blow away—she was siphoned away by me. I expelled what animated her, like squeezing water out of a damp towel. What remained? An object, a thing, a problem to solve. *I killed Stacy. Dead.* That idea swirled in my mind, and I knew I was spiraling down into one of my fugue-like states. *Stop it,* I thought. I couldn't get stymied by the weight of the whole thing. There would be time to deal with it later, if I made it that far. *This is a task, nothing more,* I told myself. *Get it done, get out.* I noticed my hands had stopped shaking.

Where do people hang themselves? I ran through an audit of movie scenes, looking for guidance, only to find that suicide by numerous other means flashed to mind. Dramatic pedals to the floor (*Thelma and Louise*), guns to the head (*The Shawshank Redemption*), redemptive acts of self-sacrifice (*Independence Day*). I thought of news stories, celebrity deaths—nothing presented itself as obvious.

No matter. I was limited in this small apartment anyway. I walked to the narrow closet next to the entrance and opened it to find several coats and jackets hanging on a bar. That looked sturdy, and she'd probably fit in there if I emptied it out. I reached in, sliding over a few items to get a grip, and pulled down on the bar. It seemed fairly solid, and I put more weight into it, giving a couple of hard, quick pulls. The bar came off on the right side with a snap. I fell with it and landed painfully on my knees and swore aloud as jackets and coats slid into a pile. I paused and listened for any signs the noise alerted attention; I looked over at Stacy. *Focus, idiot, she's not waking up*. I rolled onto my side and rubbed my knees. Both hurt, but the right one had taken the brunt, and I winced with pain when I touched it. This wasn't going to work. I stood up slowly, keeping more weight on my left, stuffed in the fallen coats, and shut the closet door. No time to clean that up.

I limped into the bedroom to confirm I hadn't seen a closet there and sat down on the end of the bed, gingerly massaging my right knee, which was starting to swell. I looked around, and my eyes fell on the two stacked books on the wardrobe cabinet, the small brass box on top of them. I read the spines: the bottom one was mine, *Giving Credit*. She had my book; why hadn't she mentioned that? Resting on top of it was *The Female Clavicle*. I reached over and grasped the brass box and opened it. Inside, beneath two thin bracelets, was a head-and-shoulders photo of a younger Stacy, perhaps as a teen, hair fashionably styled and cut shoulder length, a conservative charcoal blouse buttoned up to the neck. The mild, almost bashful smile, the clear eyes and open face: it looked like a wholesome, alternate-universe version of the Stacy I had met—someone who went to the prom, not a bipolar drug addict. It was difficult reconciling the two.

I abruptly closed the box and put it back, but not on top of the two books, as if her contact with them had created an intrusive and lurid intimacy that was intolerable. I was overwhelmed by exhaustion. I just wanted to rest, to stay in the apartment indefinitely and not face anyone, holed up and protected from the outside world. Maybe I could lie down, take a brief nap, at least. I stooped abruptly, ignoring the stabbing pain in my knee. *Get moving, fix this.*

Realizing how badly I needed to empty my bladder, I returned to the bathroom. As I urinated, I looked at the door and thought, *That looks pretty sturdy*. I flushed and stepped to the door and swayed it open and closed. It opened to the inside. The wood seemed heavy and solid—not cheap compressed wood, but quality oak or, at least, a decent pine. Probably left over from the good workmanship of the building's better days. I grabbed the doorknob on the inside and shook it; it was firmly screwed into the wood. I did the same on the outer doorknob. I pressed down on it hard this time, adding most of my weight and ready for a repeat of the closet fiasco, but it held up well. The door joints creaked ever so slightly but did not seem to loosen at all. And the door was fairly tall. I didn't have time to explore further, and what was there to discover at this point? *This is it. This is where it will be.*

I returned to Stacy's body, squatting down by her head and shoulders. I rolled her over to her back again. Her tongue had slipped back in her mouth and one eye was half shut in a partial wink. I slid my hands under her armpits. They were warm and sticky with dampness. Still in a squatting position, I slowly tugged her toward me, the tied cord trailing under her frame. She slid along, and I skirted back a step and pulled again. After ten pulls, we had reached the hall, in front of the bathroom door. I slid my arms out and wiped them on the sides of my pants. Her antiperspirant scent competed with stale body order and the sourness of urine. I walked back to where she'd lain and felt the rug for dampness. There was a bit, but not enough to attract attention, I thought. It would dry out soon enough. I leaned down and smelled the area. The trace of urine was there, but one would have to sniff around to encounter it.

I went back to Stacy and propped her up, positioning her against the hallway wall as close to the bathroom door as possible, careful not to get the cord stuck. Her head slumped forward, accommodating me with easy access to the back of her neck. The cord was still firm, with a few inches of space between the neck and the ugly joining knot. I gathered the extension cord in both hands and tossed the end over the top of the bathroom door. I looked it over and figured I would need to pull about four feet to the inner knob to loop it around and tie it off. This would really test the door. I didn't know if it would work, but it was my only option. From the inside of the door, my feet braced along the bottom of it, I slowly pulled the cord until the slackness was gone. I glanced around the door. Stacy's head was no longer slumped, but level. I would need to pull down until her feet were lifted, fast and strong in a semi-squat, then loop it around the knob very quickly. This was going to be a challenge. Maybe I could do this in one long pull. I centered myself, took in some breaths, wrapped my hands high up on the cord in a firm grip, and pulled down, putting all my weight into it. God, she was heavy! Was I really this out of shape?

My arms strained and burned with the pull, my lower back did something I knew I'd feel later, but I got my arms down to the knob and started looping as quickly as I could before I weakened and dropped her. One loop, two loops, around some more, then—what the hell was that?

Someone was knocking, a pattern like a quick drum. *Shit!* Someone finally heard me. I froze. Strangely, the knocking sounded closer than the living room. I knotted the cord as fast as I could, fully expecting it not to hold when I let go, but, to my surprise, it did; the knot tightened with the weight. I quickly stepped out to the hall to listen more closely, but the knocks were right in front of me.

Stacy's eyes were bulging, her tongue was protruding fully and her face was beet red. The knocks were coming from her tapping feet, dangling several inches from the floor, the heels bouncing off of the wood of the door as her legs mimicked a scampering walk. *Alive. How can that be?* I froze again. Was she conscious? Could she see me? Was this some sort of nervous system reflex? I couldn't move. I was completely paralyzed and fixated on her face. The bulging eyes were now red with broken vessels, the face swollen like overripe fruit, the tongue impossibly large and bluish. From behind, the pull of the cord was pushing her ears out, making her look cartoonish. The tapping of her heels against the door slowed. Then, in a blink, stillness. The legs had stopped. I stood there several more minutes, fixated, expecting a sudden movement, a scream, an accusation, a pointed finger. But nothing like that occurred. She was perfectly still. I was perfectly still. The world had stopped on its axis. Time was frozen. It was almost serene, until I looked more closely into her dead, red eyes and instant alarm seized me.

I shattered the stillness with a mad dash into the living room, driven by primal fight-or-flight instincts. All that mattered was leaving. My brain stem was shouting, *Get out, get out, get out!* I grabbed my jacket, moved to the door, and paused to listen. I looked out of the peephole. The hall was empty. I opened the door quickly, stepped out and shut it quietly, turned to go to the stairs past the elevator and froze. *How the hell could she have hanged herself? I didn't put a stool or chair by her! What an idiot!*

Was I locked out? I turned the knob and pushed; the door was unlocked and I stepped back in, ran to the living room, and looked at the chair I'd sat in earlier. Too cumbersome. The step stool—that was perfect. I ran to the kitchen and grabbed it, then set off to the bathroom door. I put the stool close to her feet, then decided to put it on its side, as if she'd kicked it. *Get out now,* my brain drummed again. It was followed by, *Fingerprints! Well, I couldn't lie about being there, so of course my prints would be discoverable. But I touched everything! Well, no time now. God, this isn't going to work. Dammit, just go!*

I ran back to the door and thought, *It was unlocked; it should be locked.* I opened it several inches and compressed the side lever of the lock so it would catch when I closed the door, then stepped out quickly and pulled it shut. I tested it. Yes, now it was locked. *Now go!* As I turned to make my way to the stairs, a group of raucous students suddenly piled out of the party next door. I stood in front of Stacy's doorway and stared at them. The group's banter quieted down as they noticed me and stared back dumbly with thick eyes and flushed expressions. I recognized a few students but couldn't place them by name; then one of them stepped forward from the rear of the group, his mouth curled in an arrogant smirk.

"Professor Waite," said Gary Fallis.

Chapter Nine

The smirk on Gary's face dissolved quickly and transformed into something resembling concern as he read the expression of alarm on mine. Before he could speak, I turned back to Stacy's door and knocked loudly.

"Please, Stacy. I'm very concerned and I just want you to acknowledge that you are okay. Please open the door." I turned to Gary. "I want you to call public safety and let them know that we have a student in distress who may be exhibiting suicidal ideation." The whole group froze, Gary among them. "Now, Gary!" I said. He blanched and immediately fumbled for his phone. I was improvising, plucking out the phrases and actions I recalled from the student wellness trainings I'd been obliged to attend.

Gary started punching in numbers, then stopped and blurted in a cracking voice, "What's the number? Somebody tell me the fucking public safety number!"

"I have it! I have it!" a young woman with a pudgy face yelled, as if shouting "Bingo." She pulled out a card from her shoulder bag and read it out. Gary tapped as each number was called. I turned back to the door and knocked again.

"Stacy, please. Come to the door. I know how upsetting this day has been. I just want to support you." Gary talked into his phone and I asked the crowd, "Who lives here? Who can locate the super with a key?" The group flustered about and the young woman who had shouted out the public safety number said, "I'll get Justin! He'll know." She quickly ducked back into the neighboring apartment, the music and voices booming out through the open door. I heard her shout in a high and full-throated voice, "Justin! Turn the music off. Turn it off! Justin! Someone find him!" The music stopped, but the loud voices continued until the chubby-faced woman yelled, "Shut up! Quiet! We have an emergency!" The chatter dropped to a murmur and a couple of drunken chuckles.

"Public safety is coming! I think they're calling the police," Gary announced to the crowd in a voice that conveyed incredulity and surprise, as if he'd just seen a magic trick. He seemed to be in shock. His head was quivering and his eyes were dilated and huge. He looked around the hall for the answer to an unknown question.

More students from next door piled out and crowded the hallway, talking over each other with questions and suggestions. The chubby-faced women pushed her way forward, towing a thin, bookish young man with black-framed glasses. "I'm Justin," he said, as if that solved an important problem.

"Do you live here?" I asked. He nodded. "Can you find the super and try to get a key to this apartment?" He turned without a word and made his way to the stairs. I knocked on the door again, then tried the knob. Thank God I had locked it when I left. A husky male student in a baseball cap jostled to the front and sidled up next to me.

"Professor, maybe we should break it down." Some in the growing crowd in the hallway grunted affirmatives and nodded. The husky student rolled his shoulders in a warm-up. *Shit.* Did I want that to happen? I wanted to control this, and I thought having public safety show up would play out well. Then again, maybe that was the wrong way to go. What if the whole scene turned to chaos? I'd already established my concern. *It's perfect,* I thought—*they can trample over everything and make a mess. Multiple hands leaving prints.*

"Gary, how long did public safety say they'd be?"

"They didn't tell me—they just said they were on their way."

I feigned thoughtful probity, then turned to the husky student. "Okay, maybe we should. Do you think you can break it down? Listen up, everyone: we can't have all of you coming it. That will only upset Stacy more, so I'm going to go in first to try to support her. Public safety should be here any minute." I doubted that; I was familiar with their bovine pace around campus. "Alright," I said, turning to the husky student. "You and I are going to try the door. If we get it open, I want you to hang back, okay?" He nodded, a soldier with a mission. We both angled our right shoulders toward the door.

"Ready? One, two . . . three!" He slammed into the door before me, taking most of the brunt, and the door cracked near the lock, but held. Before I could line up to give it another go, he stepped back and gave it a strong kick with his leg. The door slammed open and bounced off the inner wall with a bang. I gestured at him with my palm up and he stood at the ready. I walked in the living room and looked around. I noticed the mostly full Corona bottle on the table beside the chair. *I should have moved that*, I thought.

"Stacy?" I said in a hesitant voice. I turned back to the open apartment door and saw a dozen faces peering in, Gary's among them. They looked like a pack of silent chimps. I moved toward the narrow hallway and called her name again. My voice trembled with the fear that she'd answer—that, somehow, she'd gotten down and would now stand as my accuser in front of all, an avenging angel back from the netherworld. But no; there she was, hanging perfectly still, her face swollen and almost unrecognizable.

"Oh my God!" I shouted. "Stacy!" That was the signal the pack needed. They rushed in and squeezed into the entrance to the hallway. Several screamed; one gasped with an audible intake; another shouted as if in anger. I looked back at them; Gary's mouth was an open circle, like he was trying to fit in a whole apple. He emitted a sound like a leaking tire and suddenly fainted and dropped forward with a thud. One student near him leaned down and cradled his head while several others rushed past me, toward Stacy's hanging body.

"Help me get her down!" I shouted. We bounced off one another as each vied for a grip on Stacy. One student stumbled and knocked into her, causing her body to bounce into a few others. Someone shouted: "The rope! The rope!" I moved in and helped the two students who were attempting to lift her frame; one of them yelled: "Get a knife from the kitchen!" I heard several pairs of feet scamper away. "It's tied in the back! I can't get it!" someone screamed. A woman next to me yelled, "Stop lifting her! I can't reach her neck!" Another responded: "Forget that! Just help get her up! Relieve the pressure on her neck!"

"Dude, it's too late for that," someone said from among those hanging back.

"I've got a knife!" shouted another, running forward and holding up a long, serrated knife like a mad killer.

"Let him by! Let him by!" I shouted. "Keep lifting so he has some slack. Go around. That's it—cut the cord!"

"Fuck! I can't cut through it! The wiring!" he shouted. "Saw at it!" someone screeched. I could hear him grunting and sawing on the other side of the door. Then, with a snap, the cord was cut and Stacy fell down on the three of us trying to hold her up. We all fell to the floor, a pile of entangled bodies. Stacy's face pressed against mine, and her protruding, swollen tongue was wet on my cheek. I almost screamed but controlled myself.

"Get her off us! Carry her to the living room!" I yelled. Hands grabbed and found purchase. Several feet kicked into me. Then, she was up. I stood and moved with the four students carrying her out, while others circled around. We placed her on the living room floor, exactly where she'd dropped when I had fatally pulled the cord around her neck.

"Move back! Give us some room." We stood and looked down at her. It was clear that nothing could be done. No one stepped forward to try. Stacy's eyes stared up, completely red and surreal. The purple tongue looked like an eggplant. By now, the small apartment was full of people, as if the whole party had moved over from next door, loud reverie replaced by somber reflection. I heard students crying, moaning, talking in whispers. Gary, revived from his faint, stumbled forward and looked down at Stacy's body. He dropped again and was caught by two students behind him. Some students stirred in the back by the apartment door, and a short, squalid man in a public safety uniform stepped in and moved toward the circle around Stacy.

Looking down at her like she was a messy puzzle, he said, "This is messed up."

Chapter Ten

"So, tell me again. What were you doing there in her apartment for, what—two hours, you said?"

The slab-of-meat detective standing across from me didn't seem like he was in a hurry to go home to dinner. He didn't seem incurious, either. His beady, penetrating eyes were set deep in a hardscrabble face. There was an inherent aggression in his manner, glossed over by a worn-out professionalism. Whether directed at me or the world in general, it was completely unsettling. I knew he knew—well, I didn't really know what he knew specifically, but I couldn't suppress the obsessive thought that, at any moment, he would violently erupt, suddenly and without warning. Then he'd cuff me and hustle me away to a small, dank room with florescent lighting and chipped paint. Bad things would happen there. I noticed his hands looked like pink, desiccated hams, calloused and itching to break things. Or maybe I was paranoid with fear. Either way, I didn't know if I had the self-control to pull this off. I wanted to run. Away, anywhere.

The scene had been chaos. After several moments looking as blank as an offline computer, the public safety officer had the basic competency to coax everyone out of the apartment and back into the hallway. The crowd had doubled in size, curious neighbors joining the students from next door. I helped him with the task. No longer using hushed tones, strained and aggravated voices shouted and competed for volume. Someone was wailing in the distance. Uniformed police plowed through the crowd, two paramedics in tow. Others were in the hall, pressing people back and down into lower floors. The loud voices receded.

I remained near the entrance, just inside the apartment, and the uniforms peppered me with shouted questions: "What's your relation to the deceased? Did you discover the body? Is she the resident?" The "deceased" reference was juxtaposed by the two paramedics examining Stacy's body with cool efficiency. After a few minutes, one of them stood and shook his head. He said to an officer, "Coroner on the way?" They collected the collapsed stretcher with synchronized movements and exited quietly. *Aren't they going to take her? Why is she still lying there?* The cord was still wrapped tightly around her neck; one foot was missing its blue sock. *Someone should cover her foot,* I thought. The exposure disturbed me; why wasn't she covered with a blanket? I was about to ask someone to cover her when a hand tapped me on the shoulder. I turned around, and two men in suits were looking at me, one beefy and hostile looking, the other a slender and bemused black man with a stylishly trimmed beard. The bemused one hung back and then turned to the hallway. The beefy one handed me a card. I read his name on it: Sean McIntyre. A detective.

"Let's step out into the hallway," he said. He turned without waiting. I followed and passed an officer busy unfurling yellow tape.

"She had a bad break-up today and she seemed really upset—it happened during my class, she's my TA—and, well, the whole class was present, so they can confirm, but I stayed with her to see if I could help, since she was clearly not doing well, and we walked awhile and then came here, you know, to discuss the class assignments and stuff, but really I was tagging along to make sure she was okay on her own. And—"

"So, when you say upset, was she expressing any thoughts about harming herself? How was she acting?"

"Well, she was bad earlier, crying, and I tried to console her. There's a picture—"

"What do you mean, a picture?"

"Ah, yes, that was when she walked out of class and I went to check on her and she was upset and crying and she hugged me and a student took a picture and it was in the *Beak*—"

"The what?"

"The *Beacon*, the student paper. It was silly, really, but, you know, it added to the whole weirdness of the day and I didn't think it was good to not keep tabs on her later, so we met up again—"

"What do you mean, again?"

"Oh, right. I should have been clearer. After the class we had coffee, but then later, after the picture was posted, we met up again and walked for a while and talked—"

"What about?"

"Different things, really. Her work, her background. She had scars on her wrist, I noticed that, and she told me she has attempted suicide as a teenager. And that just made me more concerned, so, even though she wasn't saying anything expressly about being suicidal or anything, I still thought it was best to stay with her for a while longer. When we got to the apartment she seemed to spiral down again, and as I was leaving she said something about just wanting to make it all stop. And—"

"You were still in the apartment when she said this?"

"Well, no. I had just stepped out and she had shut and locked the door. That's when I thought I should go back in and follow up. But she wouldn't answer, so—"

"How long were you out in the hall? Before you broke in."

"Umm, you know I'm not sure. It was all pretty distressing, so I lost track of the time, but I would guess I was out there for maybe fifteen minutes?"

"You stood in the hall for fifteen minutes and what—knocked?"

"Well, no—I mean yes, I knocked, but not just knocked. I called to her and then waited a while, thinking I could give her some time, and then I'd knock again. That went on until the students next door came out. At that point, I was getting alarmed and decided to get public safety involved."

"You weren't alarmed earlier?"

"Well sure, but—" My phone vibrated and I looked at the screen. Abbie calling; she'd be home at this point.

"Can you hold on a minute, please? I need to speak to my wife."

He gave me a slight nod and stood motionless, planted deep. I stepped away and down the hall and answered the call.

"Abbie," I said.

"Danny! Where are you? It's late and you're not here."

"I'm at Hardiman. Listen, Abbie. Something terrible has happened." I paused and took a breath. "My TA killed herself."

"What?" she said. "My God. How? Where? Are you there? What are you doing there?"

"It's hard to explain it all now. I'll be home pretty soon, I think. I have to finish up with the police."

"The police?" she cut in. "Danny. What is going on? Why are you at Hardiman talking to the police? How are you in the middle of all this?"

How was I going to explain this? *Well, the truth is, I was with Stacy in her apartment, after we went for a walk, and then I strangled her to death because she was screaming after I choked her to unconsciousness. Then I made it look like a suicide. But I think the detective I'm speaking to doesn't buy it and is about to arrest me—or pistol-whip me in a locked room.*

"I know, it all sounds crazy. But, please—I'm pretty shook up. I'll tell you about it later. I just want to finish with the police so I can get out of here. This whole thing is—I mean, she killed herself, for Christ's sake. I saw the body." Abbie was silent on the other end.

"That's horrible," she said quietly. "Come home, Danny." She ended the call. I turned back and the detective was speaking with his partner, who still looked bemused. He mumbled something I couldn't hear, then walked toward me.

"Okay, I appreciate you answering my questions. I'm sure this was all very traumatizing," he said flatly, like he was ordering his usual from a menu. "My partner will escort you out. We'll probably have some follow-up questions for you, so expect to hear from me. You can call if you think of anything important." He turned away and went back into the apartment. He was done with me. His partner stepped over to me and guided me to the stairs with a hand on my shoulder.

"It's pretty damn crazy out there, just so you know. One of the officers will drive you to your residence. Some press has shown up, a large crowd of spectators—students, I suppose. Best to just scoot you in the car and get you on out of here." We made our way down several flights of stairs. As we landed on each floor, we had a view to the hallways. Heads were poking out of doorways. Some would retreat back in when they saw us, engaged in an absurd game of peekaboo. As we spilled into the lobby, lights were flashing and voices droned from outside like a loud, buzzing engine.

"Let's go right to the patrol car on the right," the detective said. We walked through the entrance and all eyes were on us. *Christ, this is surreal,* I thought. I saw strobing colors, news vans, camera lights on newspeople, one looking practically orgasmic as she spotted me. She was shouting something and then pointing her microphone at me. Another stood next to her. He looked like a wax figure and, when he opened his mouth, his teeth were impossibly white against the spray-tan complexion of his face. I couldn't understand either of them.

"I can't hear you!" I shouted, pointing to my ear and then flapping my hand in a ridiculous mime. They waved their mics more vigorously and shouted louder, further excited by my response. The detective hustled me along.

"Let's just get you in," he said. He got to the car promptly, and he opened the rear door for me. I slid in quickly, before he could place his hand on top of my head, a gesture I'd seen a million times when perps were being taken away. He shut the door without a word and waved the car away. In order to get out, the policeman had to make a three-point turn. As he did so, I sat in the back, staring out the window. Dozens and dozens of eyes were on me. Some were the students from the party, but many others seemed to have come from neighboring University buildings.

I translated their gestures and expressions into phrases: "Who is that? Did he do it? That's a professor, right? What's he doing here? Why are they taking him away?"

A rap on the car window startled me, and a camera light flashed brightly, temporarily blinding me. I rubbed my eyes as the car pulled away. As my vision cleared, I looked back to the taped-off crowd. Right at the edge, straining to keep eye contact with me, was Gary Fallis. I couldn't look away from him. I was mesmerized by his face, conveying animal hatred. Our eyes stayed locked until the distance of the car broke off the contact. I turned to the front and mumbled my address to the officer in a voice that sounded strained to me. My bowels churned, then sought relief with a fart. I apologized to the officer. He cracked his window and drove on in silence.

Chapter Eleven

"I do not understand! Why were you there?"

We were in the kitchen. I leaned against the counter with my arms locked low on my torso, carrying an invisible sack. Abbie stood a few feet away, squared off and locked in, an immovable gatekeeper granting me no passage. But there were tremors forming beneath the exterior, and I was delicately stepping around the fault lines. It wasn't going well; as in so many of our arguments, we were stuck in a perpetual loop, stating the same things over and over again and hoping they'd somehow land differently with each utterance. All the while, images of Stacy intruded on my mind, throwing me off, my own personal Banquo. Did I smell her on me? Smells were actually ingested particles, I'd read somewhere. So, pieces of her were here, in the room, in some fashion, as I argued with Abbie. I half expected her to tap me on the shoulder.

"Again, I was there because I was tagging along with her, keeping an eye on her—I told you." *Stacy's hanging feet scampering against the bathroom door.* "Yes, you're right. I should have walked her over to the Student Wellness Center, but, you know, that's hindsight."

"No, it's sound thinking, which you evidently didn't have for whatever reason."

"What's that supposed to mean?"

"What do you think? You're wandering around with a student you were hugging in public—that was great to see—and then you were in her apartment because, you say, you were concerned about her. Concerned!" she said, the word stated as evidence of something unseemly. *Stacy staring at me with flaring nostrils, itching to wrestle.*

"I was. For good reason, it turns out. Abbie, it just happened the way it did. And I can't help the fact that some idiot took a photo of us." *Stacy, prone, extending her hand to show me the photo from the* Beak. "And what does that matter now? I mean, that's kind of insignificant given everything, don't you think? She hanged herself and I couldn't stop it." *Stacy, telling me to wait, just wait.*

"Look, I know. I'm not minimizing how totally upsetting and shocking that must have been. It's tragic that she took her life." *I pull the cord and hear a crunch.* "I'm just trying to understand it all. It's just, of all people, for you to be in the middle of all this—"

"What do you mean, me of all people?"

"Come on, Danny! You've barely been making it out of your office to teach class, and all of a sudden, you're at the center of a suicide and all this other drama. You suddenly find inspiration and it's to try to play the savior for an unstable student."

"Do you think I wanted to be in all this drama, as you put it? And why does this have to be the same conversation we've been having over and over again about my motivation? Really, that's got to be a part of all this?"

"Isn't it?"

"Well, apparently it is, because you make everything about that. For fuck's sake! Between you and Paul—"

"Well, you don't do anything! You're disengaged all the time, can't seem to get excited about anything. And now you're at the center of . . . of all this! Reporters called here! A police car dropped you off!"

"I'm sorry I embarrassed you. Again." *Stacy, trying to speak, but instead her fat purple tongue flopping around.*

"Danny, don't. Just don't. I can't take you turning this around and playing the victim in all of this. I want to know what happened."

"You keep asking me what happened and I keep telling you. You're worse than the detective questioning me."

"A detective was questioning you? Why? What was he asking?" *Her bloated face asking why.*

"Yes! Of course he asked me questions. I was there; that's his job."

"But what was he asking? Did he seem suspicious?"

"Why would he be suspicious? You're the one sounding suspicious."

"You're the one acting suspicious."

"That's ridiculous," I said, sounding, to my ears, very suspicious.

"Oh, sure—it's ridiculous. That's your answer to everything! It's all fucking ridiculous!" she said in a loud, rich boom that set me on my heels. *That's ridiculous, Daniel. Cut me down, Daniel.*

"Stop it!" I yelled, surprised by my own, matching volume. Who was I speaking to? Abbie was briefly taken aback. I'd never been a yeller. She moved in and grabbed both of my arms and held her face inches from mine. "Tell me what the fuck is going on!" she shouted.

I pushed her away, harder than intended. She stumbled back and lost her balance, falling to the floor in a sitting position. She looked at me, perplexity competing with surprise, then with something resembling fear, not a familiar emotion for her. Not unfamiliar to me, though, and I was quickly taken by it.

"Oh, no—that was—I'm sorry!" I reached down to her, tentatively. She scooted back, then stood. Her eyes welled.

"Oh my God!" she said. "You bastard! Keep away from me. Don't touch me." *Don't touch me, Daniel.* She stood and retreated to the bedroom. I heard the door slam and I walked over to it.

"Abbie. I'm sorry. It was an accident, a reflex. Are you all right? Please, let me see."

"Get the fuck away from me! I mean it! Go!" she screamed. I retreated from the door and went back to the kitchen. I leaned back against the counter, then sank to the tiled floor and thought, *What is happening to me?*

In the darkness of the living room I lay on the carpet on my back and stared up at the void. I looked at my watch: 2 AM. I could not settle my mind. For the past few hours, I had been taunted by a slideshow of every blunder in Stacy's apartment. I was sure that damning signs were everywhere, gathered by crime scene analysts who'd seen it all before, the same stupid mistakes and telltale maps, all leading back to me. The detective wasn't fooled. At any moment, there would be loud knocks on the door and I would be taken away in cuffs. Abbie would come out of the bedroom, vindication in her eyes, every suspicion about this man she'd thought she knew, this animal who had pushed her to the floor, confirmed. She would thank the police.

Abbie. How could I have pushed her? I played it over and over in my mind. It wasn't intentional; it was just a reaction. And the floor in the kitchen had always been slippery. Why couldn't she see that it was an accident, like bumping into someone on the street? I'd never seen that look on her face before. It passed in an instant, but it was unmistakable. It was the same expression of animal fear that I'd seen on Stacy's face. It was a contagion, passed by Stacy to Abbie through me, the carrier. I had to wipe it away, this thing infecting us.

I walked to the bedroom and quietly opened the door. Abbie was on her side of the bed, facing away and very still. Too still to be sleeping, as if she were holding her breath. I gently climbed into my side and under the sheets; she didn't stir. I reached over and placed my hand on the small of her back, a tentative feel, the slightest of contact, as if testing something that might be too hot to the touch. She still didn't stir, so I let it remain there. The tension in her body hummed.

"I'm so sorry, Abbie," I whispered. "It was just a reaction." She was still. "I love you so much. I'm a mess and I'm scared, and I need you. I would never, ever harm you. You know that, right?" My voiced cracked, and I was surprised by the dampness on my cheeks. I felt Abbie's back loosen a bit, and I put my hand on her shoulder. I moved in closer, wrapping my arm around her, and she allowed me to take her hand. We both lay still, spooned in and hesitant to make any movement that would disrupt our tentative and essential respite.

Chapter Twelve

Stacy's phone! I bolted upright in bed and looked to Abbie. She wasn't there. I collapsed back. Stacy's phone. I had knocked it out of her hands. Where was it? How had I missed it when I was surveying the area? I exhaled and tried to center myself. I suppose it didn't really matter where it was. It wasn't like it would be more incriminating than anything else in the apartment, which had been trampled on by hordes of students. *But the texts!* She'd been texting all afternoon and evening, to Gary, I'd assumed. If so, he had them and there was nothing I could do about that for now. I looked at my watch: 8 AM. I had no memory of falling asleep, and my body was stiff from tension and exertion. I did recall a brief dream in which I was knocking on a window, trying to get the attention of an unusually large white cat. My right knee throbbed painfully when I rolled out of bed and stood. I felt like I'd been through a war.

I walked into the kitchen, filled a glass of water from the faucet, and drank it down ravenously. Warmish, with a chemical aftertaste—it was the best water I'd ever had. I walked stiffly into the living room and retrieved my phone from the floor. Four voicemails and multiple texts, one from Paul, none from Abbie. I checked the voicemails: two were University numbers, one was from Paul, the last one I didn't recognize. I would listen to them later. I needed to think. I needed caffeine.

I popped in a Keurig pod and brewed a cup, quickly downing two gulps. Then I grabbed my iPad and sat down on the couch. *It was all a dream*, I thought. I'd log into my class site, have lunch with Paul later, and veg out in my office in between. Just another day after a very bad and psychotic night. I knew this wasn't true, of course, but the idea of it was necessary medicine, if only for a brief period of self-delusion. I was certain my life was over. I could sit on this purgatorial couch for a little while, but who was I kidding? We've all seen this movie. I was going to hell, and the avenging Detective McIntyre would be dragging me there with his giant, meaty hands.

I picked up my phone and listened to the voicemail from the unrecognized number. "Mr. Waite, this is Detective McIntyre calling." Of course it was. "Can you please return my call at your earliest convenience? I have some follow-up questions." Sure, like "Would you like to turn yourself in so I don't have to come get you?" *Well, I'm not*, I decided. *I'm not going to make it easy for you.* What all this would do to Abbie—the thought of it made me sick. *Well, honey, you wanted me to be less passive.* Gallows humor.

I looked at Paul's text before listening to his voicemail: "Daniel, how terrible. Are you okay? Look at the *Beak*, if you haven't already—and call me!"

Oh, Christ. Thanks, Paul. I really needed another portrait of me as the scandalous professor run amok, satirized and vilified. *What the hell, I might as well embrace it, resign myself to my new life of infamy.* I went to the site on my iPad. The first item: "Graduate Student Stacy Mann Found Dead in Apartment, Apparent Suicide." I read on: It was short on details, but the broad strokes were there. I was named as the person who discovered the body, along with several students, after expressing alarm in the building and seeking assistance. It mentioned that she'd been found hanging from a door, that those on the scene tried to resuscitate (we didn't). Some quotes from traumatized students on the scene, followed by a copy of the email that had gone out to the student body from the vice president for student affairs. It was the usual template of generic concern and empathy, listing the same catalogue of available resources itemized in every previous student suicide email, but with Stacy's name inserted. Christ, couldn't they try to mix it up a little?

Right below—of course—was the picture of me and Stacy from yesterday. *Wonderful*, I thought, *here we go*. But I had to read the headline a few times to see if I was comprehending clearly: "The Campus Needs More Citizens Like Professor Waite." It was an opinion piece by the *Beak*'s editorial board. I read it.

The stress culture of this University claimed another victim last night; one more student ill-served by the administratively lax and unresponsive wellness culture on this campus. How many students must we lose before the administration wakes up to this epidemic permeating our students? How long before they cease with the assurances that the University is doing everything it can to support the mental health of all?

One member of our community was not blind to this. One member of our community did what he could to help a student in distress. The *Beacon* owes Professor Daniel Waite an apology— and we need to confront our own culpability in the apathy that enables the stress culture permeating all. Yesterday, our Campus Sightings column satirized Professor Waite's intervention with Stacy Mann, who took her life last night. What we should have done is follow his example. We, as a community, should have also intervened, asked ourselves how we could help. But we did not. We ignored the signs and treated them like a laugh line. However, Professor Waite did intervene. Even in light of the ridicule placed on him yesterday, he kept up his diligence and care for his teaching assistant to the end. In fact, he tried to intervene and prevent her death when no one else was listening, when—in fact—no one else was there for her. That he was too late is not a reflection of his commitment, but it is a reflection of the lack of ours. We all need more citizens like Professor Waite, and we mourn with him on this sorrowful day.

I read it again, more slowly. *What the hell?* I was being lauded. Me. I read it again.

Each step on campus was tentative, as if my feet would puncture the delusion that I was this paragon of empathy and action. I still did not believe that the idea from the opinion piece would hold. Surely, it must evaporate at any moment. Someone or something would pierce through this fraud, and my fall into hell would continue, perhaps with even more fury and condemnation. As I entered the usual path to my building, head down and trying to be a shadow, my name was called: "Danny!" I looked up to find Roger Croup's lanky frame in my way.

"Danny," he said, like the word was a pronouncement of terminal cancer. "Oh, man." He moved in and hugged me firmly, patting my back. "You did what you could. Thank you for that. I'm so sorry you had to go through this. I should have known. I should have done something." Alarmingly, he started to cry. *Dear God*, I thought. I embraced him awkwardly.

"Hey, it's okay. Roger, how could you have known? I mean, if she hadn't had that breakdown in my class, I would have been clueless. I didn't do anything remarkable. I just happened to be there."

"No! Danny, you're wrong. You did what we all should have done. You did. The weight of that, oh man—to carry that around . . . " He starting crying again. Where was his young fixture of a bride? Now, when I actually needed her, she was absent? We talked a bit more—mostly me comforting him—and I finally extricated myself. As I approached the entrance to my building, a group of students loitering outside stopped to look at me with . . . what was that? Reverence? I cautiously strolled up to them; a few offered thanks and asked how I was, and soon all began snapping their fingers, the new affirmation of support that seemed to have replaced applause.

"Thank you. Really, thank you so much," I said humbly. "I can't tell you how much your support means." No, really, I couldn't. I made my way past them and took the elevator up to my office floor. I passed a gauntlet of colleagues and students with similar expressions of support and admiration, until finally I was in the safety of my office, door shut and locked. I collapsed into my chair and checked my phone. Still no messages from Abbie. As soon as I placed it down, it rang.

"Hello, this is Daniel," I said.

"This is Detective McIntyre," he said in a hoarse monotone.

Chapter Thirteen

"So, were you both using marijuana last evening?" he asked.

"I wasn't, no," I answered too quickly. "She said it was medicinal. I wasn't surprised, frankly, given her agitation. But I didn't want any. Those days are long gone for me."

"What do you mean?"

"What? I mean, when I was young, yes. But no, I don't use marijuana—haven't for years."

"Do you drink?"

"Well, yes. Some. Not, you know, a lot."

"Were you both drinking that evening?"

"I did have a beer or two. She did as well. It was social drinking."

"Social drinking." His tone suggested I had just said something bizarre. "So, she was drinking beer and smoking marijuana and you were just drinking beer. Do you recall how many beers she had?"

"No, not really. I wasn't keeping an eye on that or counting."

"Would you describe her as intoxicated? Was she slurring her words?"

"You know, not really, now that you mention it. I think she was so agitated that it wasn't impacting her that much. At least it didn't seem that way to me. I don't remember thinking that she was drunk. Frankly, it probably would have been better if she was, a bit."

"What does that mean?"

"I just mean that maybe she would have been calmer? I don't really know what I'm talking about here."

He was silent on the line. The silence made my chest flutter.

"Hello?'

"Yeah, thanks. I'll follow up if I have more questions."

He abruptly ended the call. My short-lived bubble of delusion had been popped. *It's all going to come out*, I thought. Did I really think I had a chance of dodging this with my pathetic attempt to make Stacy's death look like suicide? I realized, with self-disdain, that I'd fallen right into the professor box, the arrogance I despised in so many of my peers, thinking I was more intelligent than those outside the Village—of course I did. After all, I was tenured at the University.

What a fool I'd been. It meant nothing; McIntyre couldn't care less. To him I was just another blundering perp, an ugly tourist in his world, tripped up by my own idiocy. Abbie's father would be vindicated. The brilliant Doctor Benjamin Stein. I had never been good enough for her. Sure, he suffered me in support of his favorite daughter, but every pleasantry, every pat on the back and word of warm banter, was permeated by an unstated disappointment. I caught his clandestine glances, assessing me like one of his lab subjects or a petri dish that had failed to produce. I was Abbie's singular failure, and he blamed himself—I could read it on his lemon-sucking face, his constant regret that he didn't intervene in time.

Still no word from Abbie. I decided to text her a brief message: *I'm around if you want to talk or meet up—whenever you want.*

Wow, that should melt her heart, I thought. My office phone rang and I picked up.

"This is Daniel."

"Professor Waite? This is Gloria Alderson, deputy to President Baldridge. Please hold for the president." The president? The most reclusive man on campus was calling my office. The man we all called Howard Hughes, the secretive fundraiser-in-chief who most certainly was on the spectrum, the stony-faced Easter Island totem who spoke but was not spoken to.

"Professor Waite?" his deputy said with a taskmaster's impatience.

"Yes, sorry. I'm here. Yes, I can speak." As if she'd been asking. A pause on the line ensued, followed by a click, followed by Baldridge's flat baritone.

"Professor Waite. Daniel, if I may."

"Yes, of course."

"Daniel. First, I want to ask how you are doing." He continued before I could respond. "The trauma of losing a member of our community is tragic enough, but to have been so closely involved, as you were . . . " (didn't I know it) "Well, I'm sure this must be a very difficult time for you. I am reaching out to Ms. Mann's family to express my condolences, and I want you to know my office is available to provide any assistance to you and your department as you navigate this terrible loss." Was he reading from a script? "Again, thank you for all you're doing to support your students and know that we all commend your efforts." There was a click, a pause, then a dial tone. I placed the phone back on the receiver.

The president, calling me to offer support and gratitude. Perhaps all wasn't lost after all.

⌇

"This is all so dizzying." Paul leaned forward and his prominent eyebrows fluttered. His hands were tapping the white tablecloth spastically. After a flood of calls and emails from various colleagues—many of whom had never acknowledged me in the past—I ran a gauntlet of professors at the faculty dining room, making my way to Paul's table for a late lunch, where he waited with the impatience of the town gossip. I was actually feeling galvanized by the constant attention, so far removed from my usual need to evade social interactions. Each affirmation drew me further from my sense of impending doom. And I was embracing this perception. Several students from my class had stopped by my office, teary and distraught, and I'd offered full-throated support, comforting them in their traumatized and shaken states. They saw me as an emotional resource, the caring adult they so hungrily needed. I'd even given the Simpleton, who came to me confused and directionless, a warm, paternal hug.

"What does Abbie have to say about all this?" Paul asked.

"I think she's still processing it all—it's a lot." *And I pushed her to the ground when we argued about it. So there's that.*

"Daniel, I have to get this off of my chest." His hands became still. "I really didn't appreciate the situation yesterday. Of course, I was concerned about the perception of everything, but had I known . . . well . . . I'm sorry for not seeing it."

"Paul, it's fine. You were looking out for me, as always. I really didn't know either. It's not like I prevented it, you know."

"Well, even so . . . " We were both silent for several awkward moments.

"President Baldrige called my office earlier."

"What? He actually spoke?"

"Well, in a manner of speaking. I think they gave him a script to read. It was bizarre, though, to hear from him, of all people."

"They're all panicking. Another suicide. You know University Public Relations is on a war footing. Have they reached out to you? They will, you know. They won't want you talking directly to the press about this, at least not until they give you talking points. Get ready!"

"I don't want to talk to the press. I definitely do not."

Here I am, I thought, *in the faculty dining room, engaged in banter with Paul. I'm discussing the press and the president, as if this were all the normal course of a day.* The surreal nature of it all. My mind flashed to Stacy's lifeless body, dragged and rolled by me, strung up by a cord by me, bloated, then kicking, then still. I was a murderer, sitting in a chair, surrounded by colleagues, and eating a salad with balsamic dressing and croutons. Later, I would . . . what, review essays? Paul was staring at me.

"You look dazed. Of course you are. It must have been a very long night."

We treated ourselves to the dessert bar. Paul had some fruit, and I had a large serving of bread pudding. We made our way out of the building and back onto the campus green, strolling in our usual post-lunch fashion, making small talk and gossiping. It was cloudy; rain seemed imminent. The normalcy was forced, but we both needed it. We parted, and I returned to the security of my office. I settled back in my chair and contemplated the blank space on the wall.

Chapter Fourteen

"Abbie," I said. "Are you all right?"

Dusk had settled in, and hard, steady showers poured outside, blurring my window. My fugue time in the office had gone on for several hours, occasionally disrupted by calls. Just as Paul had forecast, public relations reached out to run me through some talking points, all as poorly crafted and generic as the email concerning Stacy's death. I told them not to bother and said I would redirect any media inquiries to them. They thanked me profusely. Afterwards, all was wonderfully quiet. The few neighbor colleagues on my floor had departed earlier, trying to outpace the rain.

"Daniel." She paused on the line. "Yes, I'm fine. I'm not totally sure how I feel, but I'm all right. This has been a lot to take in."

"Abbie, I'm so sorry. Please, you have to understand that I didn't mean to push you like that. It was a reflex. Did I hurt you at all? God, if I did—"

"No, no. I'm not hurt. Not physically. It was very upsetting, Danny. You, of all people. I just never would have expected it. But I've had some time to reflect. I know yesterday was highly unusual and traumatizing, so I suppose I shouldn't be surprised that it would spill over to us. And maybe I pushed you too hard—"

"Abbie, no—"

"I did. And we both understand why. But it's okay. I think we need to just go easier on ourselves, for the time being, anyway." There was a remoteness clinging in her voice.

"I agree. It's been unreal. Do you want to meet up and leave for home?"

"Danny, I'm staying with my parents tonight. Don't take it the wrong way. I'm not as angry and upset as I was—I just think the breather will be good for both of us. And I'm pretty exhausted."

"I . . . sure. No, I get it. As you think best. I want to see you, of course, but I understand."

"And you will see me. It's just one night. It will be all right." We were silent for a few moments, and then she said, "That was quite the piece in the *Beak*. They did owe you that apology."

"Well, I guess. I think we're both surprised by this portrayal of me as some kind of model of responsibility." She didn't answer. "I'll be home later if you want to call. If not, I understand. I can't wait to see you."

"Danny. Take care of yourself, okay? You've been through a lot. We'll talk later. There's some food in the fridge."

"Thanks. Okay, good. Bye. I love you."

"Bye, Danny." She disconnected.

The thought of being home in solitude was both disheartening and frightening. My mind, no doubt, would be intruded on by unwelcome visitors. As I ruminated on this, there was a soft knock on my office door. I came around my desk and opened it.

"Professor Waite," said Gary.

He stood in the doorway with stooped shoulders. His face was drawn and pale, his eyes puffy and drooped. He was in the same clothes as last night, and I could smell the wet staleness on him. I didn't see an umbrella, just a messenger bag hanging loosely from one slumped shoulder, and the downpour had soaked him through. The sizable puddle at his feet made me wonder how long he'd been outside my door before knocking.

The hatred I'd read on his face the night before was gone, replaced by a vulnerable stupor. He looked at me blankly.

"Gary, please. Come in, sit down. What a terrible night it must have been for you."

I shut my office door as he sat in the chair across from my desk, dropping his bag to the floor. His motions were slow and deliberate, as if any sudden or quick movement would topple him. Despite my inherent dislike for him—and my anxiety around his connection to Stacy—I couldn't help feeling some empathy with him.

"Gary. Thank you for all you did last night. I just wish we'd gotten to her sooner. I can't help but blame myself. I never should've left her alone in the apartment."

His head was stooped as he listened. After several uncomfortable moments, he lifted it and looked at me. I was about to speak again when he said, barely above a whisper, "What happened?"

I didn't know if this was a rhetorical question or referred to something specific. Was I supposed to answer? I was about to repeat something generic and supportive again, but he blurted, "Why were you there?"

"Well, after she got so upset, I just didn't want to leave her alone," I said, repeating the gist of what I'd said to McIntyre, trying to sound calm, paternal. "She really didn't seem like she was in a good way."

"Not in a good way," he said, repeating the phrase like it was a rote language lesson. He looked directly at me, a question in his eyes probing through the stupor. My armpits began to dampen.

"No, she wasn't. I mean, you were there. In class." He didn't respond. The skin on my neck prickled. "Even after she ran out of class, and we talked, I still didn't—"

"We were very close," he cut in. "Stacy and I." He pronounced it as evidence of something conclusory. He straightened in the chair and hugged himself with crossed arms. I waited for him to speak further, but he said nothing. I noticed it was getting dark out and turned on my desk lamp. The rain continued to come down hard and thick in a windy torrent.

"I kind of knew that. She mentioned that you were friends. And you seemed to know her when she was in class yesterday. I could see how you were concerned about her."

He released a clipped, bitter laugh.

"Yeah. Friends." He drifted off, looked at the foggy, battered window. After a few moments, he looked back at me and said, "How about you? Did you *know* her, Professor Waite?" Something shy of the familiar Gary smirk had returned to his face, but it was weighed down with bitterness. My attempt at calm was evaporating quickly as I felt the cusp of a threat.

"No, Gary. Not really. We'd just met recently. But she was my teaching assistant, and I felt responsible for her. We were going to be working together."

"What an opportunity for her," he said flatly. My fist tightened reflexively under the desk.

"Gary, you are understandably upset. I am, too, frankly. There's no right way to deal with the grief and the shock, but I don't think we should poke at each other, okay?"

He smirked again.

"Poke," he said, like the word needed to be spit out of his mouth before he choked on it. "That's an . . . interesting choice of words."

"Is it?" He didn't respond. His face was waking up; color returned to his cheeks.

"What did you think of Stacy's film?" he said. Then, before I could answer: "What did you think of her weed? Pretty good, right?" The rain drummed the window loudly. We both stared at each other for several beats.

"What is this, Gary?"

He sat silently for a few moments longer, then reached into his pocket and pulled out an iPhone. I immediately recognized it as Stacy's. He held it up and gave it a brief wave.

"This is what it is. I picked this up last night, on my way out of her apartment. It was just lying there on the floor, near the corner. And I wanted to have something of hers." He cradled it in both hands; his face tremored and he seemed on the verge of tears, but then pulled back. "Yeah, we were close. We shared a lot. Like her passcode," he said. My heart pounded in my chest and ears. He tapped the phone's screen.

"Gary. I know she was texting you while I was with her. She told me. I encouraged her to. You were another connection she could make, and I wanted her to be in touch with friends," I said, nervously overexplaining.

"Actually, no. She only texted me once, after I texted her to see if she was okay. All it said was: 'Not now. Later.'"

I wasn't able to mask my surprise in time, and Gary continued. "No, she wasn't texting me. But she did enter some really interesting stuff in her Notes app, under the heading DW. That's you, by the way. Daniel Waite. Hey, would you like to hear some?"

"Gary," I said, but nothing more followed. I couldn't move or speak.

"Let's see." He scrolled through the screen. "'DW is opening up. He's talking about hating the University.' 'DW is trailing along like a lost puppy, evidently nowhere to go. I'm going to lead him home and start on him. Try to break through his lame passivity.'" Gary scrolled further down. "Here's an interesting one: 'DW is vaping my weed. I practically shoved it in his mouth. He's so pliable! I know I can break him out of his stupor.' There are others, but this is the one that I keep returning to: 'LOL. It's on! I hit him twice. Awake now! I'm . . . '" He paused, then put the phone back in his front pocket. "It just stops there." He stood and leaned on my desk with his arms, looming over me. "Why does it just stop there?"

I didn't answer. I was too stunned by what he'd read. Stacy was breaking me—what the hell did that mean? *My God*, I thought. It was all some strange game, a weird ritual. I hadn't been paranoid, after all. Was I chosen? Was it all planned—all of it? The heat rose throughout my body and my fingers twitched. What a fool I'd been.

"I know something happened there last night," Gary continued evenly. "You're a fucking fraud. You're a fucking fraud and I'm going to make sure everyone knows it. That bullshit about you in the *Beak*, like you're so fucking noble." His face turned red and his volume increased. "What did you do there? You did something to her! Tell me what happened! What did you do! What did you do to my Stacy!!" he screamed, his spittle landing on my face.

I grabbed Oliver Stone as I rose and brought it down in a fast arc, directly onto the crown of Gary's head. The impact jolted through my arms and shoulders and into my torso. A spray of liquid fanned out and spattered my desk and face; a droplet landed in my left eye, clouding it. I rubbed it, stood and looked at my hand. Blood. Gary arched back as if playing a game of limbo. He swayed back up and his eyes were wide and confused, looking for an answer somewhere on the wall beyond me. He let out a slow, two-toned moan, high followed by low, then quickly collapsed to the floor between the chair and the desk. I scurried around to him and kneeled. The top of his head had a prominent indentation the precise size and shape of Oliver Stone. *Like someone removed a scoop of ice cream*, I thought. The rain battered the window with fury, demanding admission.

"Oh no," I said.

Chapter Fifteen

*S*hit, shit, shit—*this can't be happening again.* I stood and tried to control my breathing. *Now what?* I squatted back down and placed my hand on Gary's neck, feeling for a pulse. I wasn't sure how easy that was to detect—I was simply imitating what I'd seen in movies. I was pretty sure I didn't feel any beats. I scooted the chair back to create more room and nudged him a few times. *With that concavity atop his head, he has to be dead,* I thought. I fought an urge to stick my finger in it; instead, I dug Stacy's phone out of his pocket and pressed the home button. It was locked, so I couldn't access the notes Gary had recited. What would I do with them anyway? I assumed they were also backed up in the cloud or somewhere, though I didn't really know one way or another. But I couldn't keep her phone here, in my office. I slipped it back into Gary's pocket. I couldn't keep Gary in my office, either. *This is an intractable situation,* I thought. *This is probably the end of the road.*

I walked over to my door and opened it enough for me to stick my head out and look up and down the hall. All was quiet. Great. How did that matter? I'd walk out of my office and do what—leave Gary there? Cancel office hours for the time being? Drape his body with something? That was ludicrous. He would start to smell—and worse than the average unhygienic professor. I had to get him out, but that seemed impossible. I couldn't just carry a body around. There was a security camera at the building's entrance— there were security cameras all around campus. I'd be recorded stumbling around like a corpse-carrying Nosferatu. Wait. Was there a security camera on my floor? I knew Facilities was mounting them throughout, but it was taking longer in the older buildings like mine, with turn-of-the-century wiring, so they hadn't been fully equipped yet. At least, I didn't think so.

I cracked my door again and casually slipped out into the hall. I strolled down it, trying to look unsuspicious as I gazed around. Just a professor stretching his legs, walking off a scholar's stiffness. I strolled back. No telltale black orbs gazing down, just the same old paneled ceiling and drab walls. I walked into my office and shut the door again. *Okay, so, what did that excursion solve?* Gary would still have been filmed coming into the building, that's for certain. I would have been filmed coming into the building. And now his corpse was in my office with a bashed-in head, and his blood splattered on my desk, on me. *Jesus, McIntyre, just come arrest me now.* I plopped down into my desk chair and stared out at the heavy rain, certain of my own defeat.

I could put him on the roof, I thought. At least he'd be out of my office. His soaked corpse would be discovered soon, though. Students and faculty accessed the roof all the time to smoke—it was a known spot for that. No one was likely to be up there during this rain, so there was that. Maybe I should just go up there myself. Scream my guilt, take the big dive, have a dramatic end to matters. I thought of the climax of *White Heat*, my favorite Cagney film. Cagney as the crazed and electrifying killer, standing on top of the massive gas tank and blowing himself up in a cataclysmic firestorm, yelling "Top of the world, Ma!" *No*, I thought. *My ending wouldn't be spectacular, just pathetic.* And with my luck, I probably wouldn't die in the fall. I'd just get brain trauma and lose my ability to speak in whole sentences. The Simpleton would visit me in the prison hospital, and I'd finally be able to relate to him.

Then the thought hit me like a forceful blow: despondent Gary, depressed Gary, very-close-to-Stacy Gary. Gary the copycat suicide.

I will drop Gary from the roof. When I said it in my mind, it didn't sound quite like the eureka moment that preceded it. But it didn't sound totally absurd, either. Here I was, once again working with limited options. I'd established that Gary's body couldn't stay in my office (as if the obvious needed to be established). I wasn't going to carry him out the front door of the building ("Hey, look what I found!"). I could stick him in a bathroom stall, but the cratered head would be a red light. No, this seemed like the only way to go. *Drop him and hope the damage masks the head injury. Christ, that already sounds ridiculous.* The whole thing would be a total crapshoot.

I slipped out of my office and walked down the hall to the stairs to go up to the roof and have a look. I climbed up the short flight to the metal door with the sign warning of no access, alarms, etc.—none of which were active, as every smoker knew. Anyone could get to the roof at any time. It was perfect for anyone wanting to take a leap. *Gary's family should sue the University for not taking appropriate safety precautions with its buildings. Outrageous.* I pushed the door open about a foot and peeked out. No one was there, of course. The rain was flooding the uneven floor shingles, and considerable pools had formed. My office was right below (it wasn't uncommon for me to see spent cigarette butts fly past my window), and I was surprised the failing old building didn't leak.

I returned to my office and surveyed my next steps. I looked down at Gary's corpse; he was fairly sleight, so carrying him wouldn't be too challenging, but I considered the blood that might track down the hall and up the stairs from my office. Basically, a roadmap back to the crime scene, unless I cleaned up well. It was bad enough I had to clean up my office.

I thought again of those cigarette butts falling outside my window. The window: that was it. I grabbed his bag and dug Stacy's phone out of his pocket and made my way back up to the roof, where I scuttled over to the ledge's wall, which was about four feet high. My feet were soaked in the little ponds of floating detritus—candy wrappers, cigarette butts, a plastic Pepsi bottle. I placed Gary's bag at the ledge and put Stacy's phone on top of it. It wasn't exactly a suicide note, but hopefully someone would make the obvious connection. I ran back inside, past my office and into the men's room.

Thankfully, the paper towel dispenser wasn't empty—a frequent status—and I grabbed up large swaths of rough, brown paper. I put one handful under the sink to wet it, when a toilet flushed in one of the stalls and gave me a sudden moment of terror. I turned to find Jack Spiers, ancient, befuddled, and black-suited, like an incompetent Reaper, staring at me through his thick glasses. I should have known; he often lingered into the night. As usual, he smelled like an overflowing ashtray. Jack was an unrepentant chain-smoker and smoked in his office incessantly, despite almost daily interventions and reprimands and a roof just steps away. And much to everyone's alarm, he was often discovered dozing off with a burning cigarette in hand.

"Jack! I thought I was the only one on the floor working," I said, feigning cordiality and lightness.

"Daniel, you're wet," he said, after several moments of brain processing. "Leaving now. Still raining, I assume? No matter." He paused at the sink, an unlit cigarette cupped in his right hand, his trademark silver Zippo lighter in his left, his fingers habitually tracing the engraved JS initials. "Were you at the last department meeting? We need to talk about Roger. He's not up to it."

Sometime in the distant past, before television and McCarthy, Jack had briefly been chair of my department, or so the rumors said. In every decade since, all successors had failed to measure up. He thought his comeback was imminent, and everyone was a potential recruit to the cause, so he haunted his colleagues, like some Ghost of Chairs Past. Everyone avoided him as much as possible.

"No, Jack. Not big on the meetings," I said. "Careful getting home." I exited with my mounds of paper towels, which he didn't even seem to register. One witness could now place me in my office late. Thank God it was Jack, who'd forget by the next morning. As I got to my door, Jack called out from down the hall: "Cleaning up?"

"What?" I said.

"The paper towels."

Shit, I thought. *Tonight, he chooses to be observant.*

"Just some rain from the window," I said. "See you tomorrow." I shut my door and stood by it for several minutes, hoping I wouldn't hear him knock with one last attempt to sell me on his campaign. Nothing. I set to the task of cleaning up the blood.

Chapter Sixteen

After collecting all the papers on my desk spotted with blood, I crumpled them into a ball and shoved them into the bottom of my trash basket, beneath other stuff. I smeared the remaining blood around with the dampened paper towels, then went over the spots again with dry ones. I wasn't sure whether I was actually cleaning it up or rubbing it into the dark wood of my desk. At any rate, it wasn't as visible, beyond a glossy veneer. It could even be mistaken for a coat of Lemon Pledge. I was doing the best I could, knowing that blood remnants would be easily detectable by a semi-competent analyst. Let's face it, if anyone had reason to investigate my office, it was over for me anyway.

The blood pooled on the rug under Gary's head was going to be trickier. I bent down and grabbed his ankles and gave a pull. He was light, and I had no problem dragging him off the rug and onto the exposed floor, where I placed a makeshift pillow of towels under his head. The bleeding had slowed to a virtual stop, but it had saturated his hair and looked like a failed henna job. *Now he's a redhead like Stacy*, I thought in passing. I examined the rug, poking my fingers into the damp areas, and then I lifted it up and checked the bottom to see if blood had leaked through. *Only in a few spots—not too bad.* Okay, I could take care of that. I rolled the rug up and stuck it in a corner of the office in a tight space between the wall and a battered aluminum filing cabinet. I balled up some of the few remaining paper towels and scrubbed the spots on the floor, then viewed my work. Nothing really visible to the eye. Abbie always joked about my dark and cluttered office, often suggesting I'd make a good candidate for a hoarders' reality show. *Thank you, God, for not making me neat.* Stains upon stains abounded; no layperson would notice faint brownish-red smears.

I turned to my last task, Gary's body. As I did, I was suddenly seized by the insanity of the event. I had murdered him, impulsively and intentionally. Did I have any doubt of my intention? Had the first blow of Oliver Stone not done the trick, was I really going to embrace the lie that I wouldn't have struck again—and again, if necessary? While the impulse showed some real stupidity of method, leaving me with a corpse in my office, I had to accept that the act came, well, naturally. The act of killing Stacy haunted me; killing Gary did not. And both actions seemed plausible to me, sound reactions to threats. But threats to what? What was I protecting, almost reflexively? My standing and position at the University? I had scorned and condemned the place—even, in extreme moments, entertained the idea I was ready to throw it all away, make a dramatic exit from academe, and flip it off with the third finger of contempt. Yet, faced with the potential for a bit of scandal, some bad public relations, I'd readily killed. Okay, perhaps not intentionally with Stacy, but certainly with Gary, though in his case it was to avoid exposure of the first killing.

I sat down in my chair. My mouth watered and I had to fight back the urge to vomit. My former safe reality had evaporated into a useless mist. I knew nothing. I didn't know why Stacy had played me, I didn't know why I was protecting my status, I didn't know why I had pushed Abbie, I didn't know why I had gone to such extremes. It simply didn't fit. I was a schlep, a spousal hire, a nice-guy beta bringing up the rear. Certainly harboring thoughts of rebellion and resentment, but, in the end, too complaisant—yes, too passive—to act on them. At least, this is who I had thought I was (though one-eyed John Costello might beg to differ). Who had I really been? Who was I now? I knew one thing: if I didn't stop marinating in my existential stew, I would be contemplating ideas of personhood in prison. *Quit this, Danny. Get on with it; you can explore your soul when you have the luxury.*

I gathered up all of the used paper towels and crammed them into the bottom drawer of my desk. I moved to Gary's body and grabbed him by the shoulders, pulling him over toward my window, where I propped him up against the lower wall. His face was a frozen mask of confused shock. I turned off my desk lamp and pulled the window shade further down. The rain was still a torrent, and I moved all of the clutter by the bottom sill—stacks of paper, books, and discarded pens that had run out of ink. I pulled the window open about a foot, and wind and rain blew in forcefully. I nudged Gary from behind and lifted him up by the shoulders and turned him around, toward the window. I pressed my body against him to pin his slender frame against the wall under the window, a disturbing intimacy that made me shiver. As I did so, I scooted him up so his head leaned toward the opening in the window. He looked like he was trying to peer out into the blustery darkness.

I looked out as well, wiping a small peephole on the foggy window. I couldn't see any evident pedestrians, but then someone scurried past under an umbrella. I waited, then paused. *Wait. Wait. No one coming down the path. Okay, do it now!* I hauled Gary up and pushed his head and torso out of the window. I slipped on the wet office floor and lost my grip on him. He remained half in, half out, and I got up and grabbed each leg and pushed. He only moved a few inches; something was stuck on the frame. I reached over and felt around. A belt loop on his pants! I fumbled with it, then pushed again, losing my balance, and out he went. My forehead banged into the windowsill painfully just as the soles of Gary's shoes disappeared into the void. I bent down and braced for the sound of impact. I thought I heard a muffled thud amidst the noise of the rainy wind, but I might have imagined it. I quickly reached up and shut the window and sank down to the floor. I sat in the darkness, too nervous to move. And I waited.

I sat perfectly still for ten minutes. I was waiting for a sign, a sound, some commotion indicating that Gary's body had been discovered. Nothing. Just the howling wind and rain. *I should leave now.* What was the point in staying? I crawled on the floor until I reached my knapsack behind the desk. I pulled out a cheap compact umbrella that had replaced a lost cheap compact umbrella, then reached up to collect my jacket, which was draped on the back of my desk chair. I wasn't quite sure what purpose crawling served, so I got up gingerly, put on my jacket, threw my sack over my shoulder, and, umbrella in hand, stood at my office door with my hand on the knob. Leaving seemed so daunting. Once I opened that door, I would be exposed. I knew my office was providing only the illusion of safety. Nonetheless, my heart thumped, and I felt short of breath as I stood there. *Just go,* I thought— *this is ridiculous.* I pulled the door open, walked out briskly, trying not to run, and made my way down the eight flights of stairs, the idea of the elevator feeling like a trap. I thought of Malle's *Elevator to the Gallows* and shivered.

I landed in the lobby and viewed the large, front entrance doors. The temptation to exit through them to confirm if Gary's body was there was overwhelming. I had the panicky notion that it wouldn't be, that he'd gotten up and walked to the public safety office to report me—injured badly, limping along, but not truly dead, a zombie in search of justice. Not so unreasonable, given Stacy's brief resurrection. I noticed the security camera installed on the lobby ceiling close to the entrance and turned to retreat down the half-flight in the rear, leading to the back exit. Christ, I probably looked incredibly guilty just then, lurking in the lobby while my internal drama played out for the camera. *What an idiot.* I pushed through the back door and stepped out onto the path. Again, I was arrested by the urge to circle around front, to get just a peek around the corner. I could stay behind one of the shrubs for cover. *No, don't be a fool. Wouldn't that be great if someone spied you lurking in the bushes?* No, that wouldn't look the least bit suspicious, what with the dead body and all. *Just exit, like a normal, innocent man, one not worried about corpses.*

I opened my umbrella and walked along the winding path, knowing I'd need to do a large half-circle to exit through the main thoroughfare. As I walked along the shadowy route, it occurred to me that the layout of the campus, with its narrow paths, obscuring bushes and gothic blind spots, was a criminal's dream. Modern security issues must not have been in the forefront when the University was constructed all those centuries ago. No wonder there were the occasional thefts, burglaries, and assaults on campus. Public safety officers were posted at the campus's bright entrances, precisely where they did the least good, occasionally making rounds (infrequently, when not supervised). I was grateful for that as I passed through the gates and gave a quick wave to the two bored officers who dutifully ignored me. I was just another academic struggling with a useless umbrella in the windy rain.

Passersby on the sidewalks scurried around, and I felt a budding sense of normalcy as I joined their queue. Faces were obscured by umbrellas, and the collective anonymity warmed me like a security blanket. The smell of wet concrete and the glitter of lights reflecting off of rain-glossed windows left me almost giddy. I felt a lightness in my step that had been absent for the last two days.

I had no sound reason to justify this blissful state. Nothing had really changed. I knew rationally that the blundering messes I'd created could still bring me down. But maybe not. Yes, McIntyre was eyeing me with aggressive and probing intent, but I was hit by the welcome thought that maybe his demeanor toward me was his default setting. Maybe it really had nothing to do with me, specifically. Hell, he probably spoke to his kids the same way, if he had any. He probably engaged the entire world with the same hardened cynicism. All, in his eyes, were guilty of something. And his partner hardly seemed to register me; perhaps I was that unimportant. Maybe they looked at Stacy's death as what it was taken by most to be: a student suicide. Gary would simply be the requisite copycat, even an act they were expecting. I imagine his relationship with her would only underscore the certainty. Yes, maybe—just maybe—all would be fine.

As I strolled along, I tilted my umbrella back and enjoyed the street view; I was refreshed by the cleansing rain against my face, and images of

Gene Kelly came to mind. I spied a tall woman about a block ahead of me, intimately tangled up with a man holding a large umbrella for two, and her loping gait reminded me of Abbie's. *Abbie*, I thought. I had a deep longing to be in her company right now. I would make it up to her. I would try to keep this buoyant mood and would show her that I could move on, that I could be the productive man she so wished I would be.

She was right—I had been a total, self-involved schlep. What right did I have to be so dreary? I had an incredible superstar for a wife. I had a ridiculously easy job at one of the most prestigious universities in the world. I was tenured. Good God, if the outside world actually knew how little tenured professors did, it would be scandalous. Stacy was right—if you had tenure, you could get away with murder. But seriously, I was actually being paid to talk and (occasionally) write about movies that I loved, and no one could stop me! In what reality was this not a wonderful life?

In my euphoric and newly enlightened state, I was skipping along so fast I had almost overtaken the couple ahead. They were still clinging to each other, and I felt a glowing humanity toward them. *How wonderful love is.* Their intimacy warmed me like an embrace. Perhaps this was simply because the woman reminded me of Abbie. My love for her felt reignited—the flame had never burned out, but I realized now how I had neglected it. I couldn't wait to see her, to share my newfound zest. *Wow,* I thought, now just steps behind the couple, *she even has Abbie's fashion sense.* It felt like a providential confirmation of my feelings to happen upon her look-alike.

Doesn't Abbie have that coat? As they turned a corner, her companion's hand reached down from her lower back and stroked her ass. At the same time, the Abbie look-alike turned her head into his and bit his ear. Except the look-alike wasn't, in fact, a look-alike. She was Abbie. And she was darting her tongue into Terry Rockford's ear. Dutiful research assistant that he was, he turned to her and reciprocated. I stopped in my tracks. They turned the corner and went out of my view.

Chapter Seventeen

"Can I get you another?" the bartender asked.

"Sure, thanks." He removed my empty glass with the smooth, polished manner of an old-time pro. He also read his customers well, knowing who to engage and who to leave alone. I was in the latter category, sitting on the edge of the bar for the past hour, staring at the glossy wood countertop. He replaced my beer unobtrusively.

After standing in the rain for several stultified minutes, umbrella lowered, I realized I was getting drenched. I'd ducked into the nearest establishment: Jimmy's, an old-school bar that was getting trendy with student hipsters keen on proving their eye for authenticity. It was fairly crowded for a weeknight, probably filled with people like me, seeking temporary refuge from the rain. I sat and contemplated the latest item on the growing list of things I did not know: Abbie.

How had this happened? Were there signs I'd missed? *Undoubtedly, you fool—what a stupid question.* I'd been so focused on my existential malaise, my navel-gazing, I seemed to be oblivious to the reality around me. Crushingly, Abbie was just one more example. I tried to stir up jealous outrage, but my heart wasn't in it. No, I couldn't really blame Abbie; my self-imposed funk was to blame. I had been pathetically clueless about, well, everything, it seemed. And it had led to all of this: Stacy, Gary, now Abbie. The shock of seeing her with Terry had punctured the joy I'd been feeling. Terry, that unctuous, smiling sycophant. I wanted to punch out all of those big white teeth. What could she possibly see in him? He was a phony, a plastic man. No, whatever this was, it wasn't serious. It couldn't be. It was a distraction, a vacation from the doldrums of her existence with me.

As thoroughly depressed as I was, surprisingly it didn't drain me of the motivation I'd felt earlier. In fact, if anything, it sharpened it. After all, when I'd killed to protect what was mine, I had taken measures I didn't know I had in me. I'd woken up, lifted the veil, and seen my life with clarity, and I was not going to let it slip away, not after all I'd done. If Abbie was fooling around with her assistant, it was because I hadn't been there for her. I'd been too selfish. That was going to change—it already had. She would see the difference, and I would win her back. I would do the work to stop all of this foolishness. And if Terry continued to be a problem—well, I'd demonstrated my determination in addressing problems. I wasn't planning on stopping now. After all, student suicide was a veritable epidemic; no one was immune, not even glossy-toothed sycophants.

Some gasps rose up from a table behind me and I turned to see what the commotion was about: three patrons, obviously students, with distressed expressions, one passing her phone around to the others. As each looked, their faces bounced from shock to puerility. I caught the eye of the one sharing her phone, and, after a brief expression of annoyance that I was looking at her, she made a comical circle with her mouth and raised her eyebrows. She nudged the hair-gelled male sitting to her right and gestured toward me. He half stood and waved at me, then made a beckoning gesture. *What the hell*, I thought. I collected my drink and walked over and sat in the empty chair.

"Professor Waite?" he said in a hesitant voice.

"Yes, hello. And you are?" I offered my hand and he took it.

"Orson. Orson Burgher. This is Alex and Greta." He gestured toward the other two, and they offered formal handshakes. Orson was handsome and well groomed in a pressed Oxford shirt; he looked like an MBA student. Alex was dark, petite and eating-disorder thin, wearing a baggy black top. Greta was a big-boned, Teutonic-looking young woman with a wide, attractive face and straight blond hair pulled back in a clip. Her denim jacket was emblazoned with a Pep Boys decal. All three had somber expressions. It was like the beginning of a comically serious business meeting.

"I took your class a few years ago, Professor," said Greta, the owner of the passed phone.

"Oh, sure! I thought you looked familiar." She didn't look familiar at all.

"So, I don't know if you heard, but given what happened last night, with your student . . . " She trailed off, not sure how to continue.

"What she means," Orson interjected, "is that we just saw this and, well—we didn't know if you were aware." He looked at me with concern and passed the phone my way. I looked at the screen and saw the *Beak's* headline: "Student Dead After Fall from Mason Hall; Suicide Suspected." *Wow, that was quick.* It occurred to me that I'd given little thought to Gary in the past hour; I could thank Abbie for that. The short article didn't name him, and nothing very factual was confirmed, but an undisclosed source alleged that there was evidence of suicide and that the student's actions were possibly connected to Stacy Mann's death. *Yes, that's a reasonable conclusion*, I thought. I handed the phone back to Orson and feigned shock and grief.

"I can't believe it. This is simply terrible. They don't say who the student is, just that there's a connection to Stacy. What can that mean? God, I hope it's not a student from my class. I don't know if we can handle that, not after everything." I lowered my head and shook it slowly.

"The thing is, Professor," said Greta, "I've been texting with some students who are there. They saw the ambulance take the body away, and one of them knew who it was. His name is Gary Fallis."

"Oh, no!" I said, perhaps a bit too loudly. Heads turned toward our table. "Are you sure? This is terrible! I know Gary; he's in my class. And he does know Stacy—did. Pretty well, I've come to learn." I looked at them. "I can't believe this."

"My friend's friend seemed pretty sure. I guess he knew him and was really upset. I mean, of course he was. Wow, this is awful. I am really sorry, Professor." She put her hand on my forearm, and Orson, wanting to be helpful, went to the bar to get me another drink.

"This must be especially hard," she continued, "given all you did yesterday. Your involvement, I mean. How you tried to help your TA. That was truly wonderful. Really, it meant so much to a lot of us." She stroked my forearm. "Are you going to be all right?" Her pink face was an emblem of concern. Orson came back with my drink, and I used it as an excuse to move my arm.

"I'll be okay, but really, to have this happen again. The class will be devastated—the whole campus will be. God. I've read about this copycat phenomenon, but for it to really happen like this. Well, it's real to me now."

"I understand." Greta scooted her chair closer to mine and put her hand back on my forearm. She looked at me with moist eyes, and it occurred to me that she was fairly tipsy. "A close friend of mine took her own life. It was devastating. I tried to help her, too—like you did. But it happened anyway. I was so upset, that I . . . well." In an apparent gesture of sadness, she leaned her head toward my shoulder, but she was too far away, so she ended up just spinning it in the air. Orson and Alex exchanged glances. Alex, stern and pensive, hadn't spoken since our introductions. I looked at Orson, a plea for help in my eyes. He raised his eyebrows slightly.

"Well, we should be going," he said. "I'm sure you have a lot to deal with." He got up from his chair. "Again, I'm really sorry. It's tragic." Alex stood too, but Greta remained seated.

"You two go. I can't go anywhere right now. I'm too shocked. I need to just sit." She looked back at me, nodding as if I understood our shared plight. Orson and Alex waited a beat, said their goodbyes, and quietly exited.

"Really," Greta asked, "are you going to be okay?"

Energetic, inebriated Greta seemed to enjoy laughing and crying in equal measure. I had yet to extricate myself. Although her sloppy extroversion was making me uncomfortable—and although the last thing I wanted to do now was sink into another student's drama—I wanted to be seen here, in public, at Jimmy's. Yes, it could be confirmed I was on campus when Gary took the plunge, but I felt I was constructing a narrative here. I was just another patron, shocked to hear news of another student suicide, along with the other patrons. And socializing at a table with someone seemed less conspicuous than sitting at the end of the bar, alone and silent. On the other hand, I was getting close to making an exit. Greta would be sitting on my lap soon, and that was not the kind of social visibility I had in mind.

But in the meantime, she was proving a valuable source of information. Her texts were a veritable news feed. Gary had been named as the deceased student. There were references to an item belonging to Stacy Mann found among his possessions. Students who knew both were coming forward to acknowledge Gary's connection to Stacy. Police were on the scene, of course, and I wondered if my nemesis, McIntyre, was on the job, surveying the scene with simmering anger. A shiver ran through me at the thought of confronting him again.

"What's the matter? You look like something just shocked you. I mean, on top of everything. What is it?" Greta asked. Her fleshy face was too close to mine, and she looked into my eyes with an expression that said *let's play show and tell*. She drank beer by the pitcher with the professionalism of a Viking, and her Teutonic genes seemed to absorb the alcohol like a sponge. I would have passed out pitchers ago. Her question created a good opening to leave. I'd been in public long enough, and her news feed was starting to taper off.

"Oh, it just all keeps hitting me. I think I'm crashing from the shock of it all. I'd better head home. I think I'll need to rest to face the day tomorrow. Thanks for listening to me." I'd barely gotten a word in, but I was leaving with knowledge of all the major milestones in Greta's life, from her first pet to her first abortion.

"No! Really? Stay!" she pleaded, grabbing both my hands. Someone called her name from the bar's entrance and she shouted a robust greeting.

She released her grip on me and jumped up from her seat. "You have to stay now! Meet these two." A pair of students walked over, staggering a bit. Greta shouted: "This is Professor Waite! Yes, that Professor Waite." They both looked at me dumbly.

"Here, please take my seat. I was just leaving." I stood and grabbed my bag and jacket.

"No! You have to stay!" Greta pleaded. She took my hand and pulled; she was quite strong. It was definitely time for my exit.

"Okay, let me run to the restroom and I'll come back, but just for a bit. Really," I said.

"Yay! Okay, hurry back!" she turned to the couple and began an animated conversation.

I walked toward the restrooms in the back, glanced over at the table, turned right and made a quick beeline for the exit. I got out onto the street; the rain had stopped and the air was refreshing. As I walked briskly away from Jimmy's, my phone rang and I looked at the screen. With sudden dread, I recognized McIntyre's number. I was about to answer it when I heard Greta's hearty voice scream from down the block: "Professor! Good news! Gary Fallis is alive!"

Chapter Eighteen

I staggered into my building's lobby after fumbling with the key. This wasn't intoxication; it was shock. My motor skills were barely functional, all of my body's energy reserves having flooded my screaming brain. It took all of the focus I could muster to not faint in front of Greta. She took my stupor for the good kind—the euphoric freeze of a moment too good to be true. *Hooray! Gary is alive! Unbelievable! Truly! No, I'll pass on the celebratory drink—thanks! I have to go dodge the cops now! Or take my own plunge! Wish me luck!*

It was impossible. How could Gary be alive? Even if the crater in his head hadn't done the trick, the fall most certainly should have. Did he land in a bush? Did the rain-soaked lawn provide a cushy landing? Was he conscious? I imagined him, in the intensive care unit at the University Hospital, barely able to struggle out words, his body twisted in pain, but determined to cough out my actions. McIntyre would be there, patiently listening as his righteous anger stored up the hellfire he would rain down on me. The police might be on their way here now.

I got off the elevator and plodded to my door. Doomed or not, I was going to lie down for five minutes. I needed to find out Gary's status to know what my next step should be, but I was on the verge of collapse. I

repeated my earlier key-fumbling routine and spilled in, dropped my bag
and headed to the coach, where I sank in. *God, this is heaven*, I thought.
I looked at my watch: 9:20. *All right, ten minutes, and then I'll come up
with a plan.* I blacked out immediately after that thought.

"Abbie!" I awoke with a jolt to find her standing over me. Did she
wake me or had she been simply waiting for me to stir?

"Danny. You were really out. I called your name when I came in
and you didn't even move." She remained standing. She had an odd look
on her face, one I wasn't familiar seeing from Abbie. She looked—sad?
Apprehensive? I looked at my watch. 11:30. I jumped up from the couch.

"I have to go!" I said.

"What? Where? It's almost midnight. Where could you possibly have
to go?"

It was a good question. Where indeed. I checked my phone and saw a
text from Paul, asking me to call him. Later. I needed to get to the hospital.
I had no idea what I could achieve there, I had no rational plan, but the
driving compulsion to be near Gary overwhelmed reason, much like my
earlier urge to peer behind the bushes to see his body. I simply had to go,
in case I had an opportunity to—I don't know—do something. At least I
could get a read on his condition. Or I could be walking into McIntyre's
handcuffs. Either way, I was hospital bound; I didn't have a choice. A force
stronger than I could resist had taken hold.

"I guess you didn't hear. There was another suicide—well, maybe
unsuccessful. It was a student from my class. Gary Fallis." I saw the
name register. "Yes, the guy who irritated me so much. He's at University
Hospital and I have to go."

"That's awful. But why do you have to go? To do what? Where you
involved somehow?"

"You mean like with Stacy? No, no—nothing like that. But they think
it's connected to her—they dated or something—and he was my student,
so I should be there."

"But—"

"What are you doing home, anyway? I thought you were staying with your parents." She tried to keep her poker face, but I could see she was startled by the accusation in my tone, and so was I, especially given my earlier feelings. But I couldn't help it. Maybe it was the knowledge that Gary was alive. Or my competing states of futility and action. Or being too worn out to pretend. Either way, I had no patience to verbally dance with Abbie right now, no time to play the cuckolded husband role, or jealous husband, whatever. Fuck it. It was stupid to ask her, and I didn't need her to answer.

"I'm going to the hospital because I need to. And you weren't at your parents, at least not a couple hours ago. We'll talk when I have time. We're going to clear this all up, and, frankly, I don't have the patience or ability to bullshit around anymore. I love you, and I'm not putting up with anything that messes with that. I'll be back when I can." On impulse, I reach out for her arms and brought her in close, then gave her a deep, wet kiss. I startled her, and her mouth was frozen, but then her tongue came to life and responded forcefully; her breathing became heavy. I broke off the kiss and backed her away. "We'll talk later. Stay home."

"Danny," she said, flushed.

"Later. Soon. I have to take care of this." I left her standing by the couch, dumbfounded, and grabbed my jacket and headed out the door. To what fate, I had no idea.

University Hospital was a University acquisition. It used to be a worn-down public hospital serving the underprivileged in the surrounding neighborhood. Now it was a worn-down private hospital serving the underprivileged in the surrounding neighborhood. And students from the University. Its architectural style was Soviet-bloc chic, with color-drained brick and thin, long windows that sapped any expectation of a brighter life outside the hospital walls. It looked like a place where one went to die from red-tape malignancy. The lobby smelled like my classroom, with an added stench of destitution. The people wandering around looked tired and violent, resigned and agitated. Someone was moaning in pain, but I couldn't locate the source. A short, Spanish-speaking woman was yelling at the reception attendant and punctuating every other word with a chop of the hands. I sidled up next to her and waiting for an opening.

"Excuse me," I said. "Can I just ask about a patient who was brought in tonight?" The woman next to me ceased chopping and looked at me with indignation, then resumed. The bored, sleepy-eyed attendant looked at me and said nothing.

"It's a student of mine—"

"Name?" she said, ignoring the other woman.

"Gary Fallis." She tapped her keyboard.

"Fallis?"

"F-A-L-L-I-S." She tapped some more.

"What is your relation to the patient?"

"He's my student. I am his professor—"

"He's in Intensive Care-Trauma Unit. Only immediate family can see him. Are you a member of the immediate family?"

"No. Again, he's my student. Is there a waiting area up there? Maybe some others are there, or a doctor I can talk to?"

"Elevators to the back and left. Eighteenth floor. Go through the double doors and down the hall. Then take a right and go through the other double doors. Take a left and the waiting area is on the right." *Jesus.*

"Thank you." I made for the back elevators, and the chopping woman continued her tirade.

The ascending elevator stopped doggedly at multiple floors, people exiting and entering to the anemic bell tone. With each stop, the dread over my compulsion to come to the hospital deepened. I was acting like one of Edgar Allen Poe's basket cases. Was I the cliché of the criminal subverting his own act out of an unconscious desire to get caught? I recalled reading an essay about that, the criminal's need to get credit for his ingeniousness. *No thanks—no credit needed here.* I was pretty sure I didn't want to get caught. But the desire to know—to know whatever I could about Gary, my success or failure, my next steps—was moving me forward.

Or more accurately, I was being chased. I was on the run from those continual revelations of ignorance plaguing every misstep and stumble that resulted in me being here, in this slow elevator, sharing passage with the assorted cast of the hospital—the ill, the desperate, the white-jacketed men and women wearing expressions of futility and professionalism. The doors opened on the eighteenth floor, and I followed out a Filipino nurse in cushioned white shoes that squeaked with each step. My brain tried to recall the labyrinth to my destination. After a few turns, it seemed the nurse was continuing ahead of me, so I gave up trying to remember and just followed her, hoping her squeaks would lead me to the waiting area.

She was a good guide. She didn't take me directly to the intensive care waiting area, but close enough that I was able to spot it. Several people were there, most sitting silently, two of them engaged with a youngish doctor, probably a resident. As I approached, the couple listened to the doctor and acknowledged what she said with slight nods. They looked to be in their fifties, casually but very elegantly dressed in crisp attire. Abbie would know the brand names. Given the hour and the circumstances, they seemed fairly calm, though the imprint of stoicism was evident on their faces. On closer inspection, one could see the emotional exhaustion of deep loss. Nonetheless, they were tan and fit. She took Pilates and yoga classes, no doubt. He looked like a golfer, maybe some tennis. They radiated money in the understated, patrician manner of the multi-generational rich. As I hovered near their perimeter, I heard Gary's name mentioned. *This must be his family.* I moved in a bit closer and, before I could find a diplomatic time to jump in, the woman listening to the doctor turned to me with an appraising eye. To my surprise, recognition seemed to animate her face. Had we met before? She rested an arm on the man's shoulder, a tactful interruption, then turned fully to me.

"I believe you're Professor Waite," she stated.

"Yes. Hello. Are you here because of Gary? I didn't mean to eavesdrop, but I heard his name." The man assessed me. His face was pleasant but probing; his eyes penetrated me, calculating all of my angles. The woman continued as he watched me.

"Yes, well. For Gary, sadly. But we were also here because of Stacy. I understand you tried to help her. I want to thank you for that—it truly does mean a lot that you tried." Her reserved tone cracked a bit, but she recovered her composure almost immediately.

"Oh, did you know Stacy? Yes, it really is terrible. I'm so sorry. Are you Gary's family?"

"Yes, he's our nephew."

"Oh! Well, again, it's terrible and I'm so sorry. He's always been one of my most engaging students. How is he, if I may ask?"

"We're waiting for more tests." The doctor receded.

"Are you able to speak to him? Is he conscious?"

"He's not. We hope he can hear us, though."

"I'm so sorry. But he's alive, so I'll keep up hope. This must be very hard. I still can't believe all this has happened. And with Stacy." They were both silent and somber. "So, did you know her? Did I understand you correctly?"

"Yes." Her face quivered, ever so briefly, and the man put his arm around her waist. She held her composure and said, "Stacy was our daughter."

Chapter Nineteen

"Anastasia was always so serious, precocious, and creative as a child. Stacy, I mean. I suppose I should call her that, since it was her preferred name of late." She brushed a fallen strand of hair behind her ear and continued: "And she was so popular at Choate. She was always one step ahead of her teachers, we were so often told. Even among those high-achieving students, she stood out. It really wasn't until her freshman year at Yale that we began to see, well, a shift."

I sat dumbfounded in the hospital cafeteria, listening to Audrey Mann tell me about her daughter. William, her husband, would nod and chime in with comments from time to time, but Audrey did most of the talking; she was the authority on the matter of Anastasia. They were from New Canaan, Connecticut. Stacy was an only child. She was an accomplished equestrian and pianist while at Choate.

This was most certainly a misunderstanding. We would quickly discern that we were talking about two very different individuals who simply shared the same name. We would laugh uncomfortably about our error and they would tell me more about this Stacy I did not know. But, of course, that was deluded. The facts connected the dots: the suicide, the awareness that I was present that evening, the expository way her narrative was a prelude for revelations about Stacy to come. So I sat and waited for the full story to unfold, knowing that the biography Stacy had shared with me was that of an anti-Stacy. Every element—the abusive father and passive mother, the broken, working-class home in Akron, the substance issues—all of it, fiction. Constructed for a purpose I did not know. The person I strangled did not exist.

"In retrospect, some of Stacy's assertive ways—her seriousness, her need to run every project, to become the savior for every cause—were chalked up to her superior leadership as a student. And people did follow her; she was a natural. She was dynamic and motivated, and she knew how to rally a group."

I didn't know what to say, so I simply continued to listen. I had no idea how to chime in that Alternative Stacy was a quasi-rehabilitated drug addict from Akron who didn't fit in well with the higher education scene, despised the establishment, and strove to break me.

"She headed to Yale ready to take over the world. She wanted to study politics, feminist theory, international affairs. She was going to pursue medicine, and also health policy. She was inspired by so many academicians and thinkers. She was so engrossed by your wife's work, all of which she burned through while at Choate. But of course she told you that. She was going to be a public intellectual like Abbie Stein, she'd say. One who had an impact. She would quote from—please forgive me, I'm forgetting the title—*The Female Crevice?*"

"*The Female Clavicle.*"

"Yes, that's it. She had a repertoire of citations from her favorite thinkers and would quote them regularly. Her memory was incredible. And she loved her first semester at Yale. When she was home for winter break, she could barely tolerate being away. And then, that spring, something . . . changed. Did we miss the warning signs? When we saw her interests shift to the fine arts, we just thought she was trying on different clothes, doing what an undergraduate should do.

"But then her passions truly seemed to alter. She became less enamored of her academic subjects and joined various arts clubs—visual arts, video, that sort of thing. She joined an experimental dance company. We came to a performance, at her request. I couldn't make heads or tails of it. No one was dancing, per se; they were walking around and jumping, making strange gestures and noises. The music was grating. I tried to hide my distaste, but you couldn't fool Stacy. Nothing got past her."

"I didn't mind it," William interjected.

"Of course you didn't, dear. You like everything." She patted his hand. "Then, she didn't come home her first summer. She went to Berlin, for what we thought was a study abroad program. But it wasn't, actually. There was some avant-garde film artist named Dieter Becker she wanted to work for, as an intern, along with a few other students from her arts clubs. Apparently, they all shacked up in his loft, where he also lived and had his studio, making films.

"Whatever happened there, that was the real turning point. She called it her awakening, but it was clear to me and William it was a breakdown. When she returned from Berlin, she was simply manic, talking about her new vision of things, her future projects. She'd shaved her head and favored black attire, which only accentuated how thin she'd become, dangerously so. And there was her wrist. The cuts were barely healed. Well, we were mortified—and concerned, obviously. She said it wasn't what we thought, that it was a 'performative act' on her body, whatever that meant. It was an artistic statement on mortality, she said.

"Performative—everything was a performance: identity, sex, all of reality, she would say. Needless to say, this sounded completely delusional. We tried to get her to see someone, and we only succeeded because of Gary. She wouldn't listen to us, of course. Thank God she still listened to him."

"So sorry to interrupt, but Gary was . . . ?"

"Gary is her first cousin. But he's really much more than that. For all practical purposes, he grew up in our home. My sister, bless her—not the most stable creature, she divorced young, after eloping with her academic tutor. Right after Gary was born she was not, shall we say, one's idea of the nurturing mother. She'd come and go, depending on whimsy and resources, and the periods away become longer with time. She was always that way, my little sister, carefree and reckless—totally irresponsible. And Gary, well, he needed the comfort, the steadiness, and we were so fond of him. And we weren't going to let the tutor raise him, obviously. William saw to that."

"Actually, my bank account did," William mumbled.

"So really, he was more like a younger brother to Stacy. They were so close, constant companions, and she simply adored him. Even though he was five years younger than she was, he was so mature. My little gentleman." She paused briefly to compose herself. "Well, Stacy did listen to him and saw a psychiatrist. I wish I could say he had an impact, but, frankly, I'm not sure he viewed matters with the same urgency as me and William. He told me to try a hands-off approach, to let her explore. Well, I'm sorry—that is simply not my nature. I may not be a physician, but I knew a crisis when I saw one."

"You did the best you could, Audrey," said William, a hand on hers. She sat perfectly still, as if any slight movement would crack the stoical façade. William checked his phone.

"She returned to Yale and formally declared as a film and media studies major. Her other interests—the academic ones—fell to the wayside, her grades suffered, and she got more involved in the arts scene, on campus and off. And she cut us off. When she finally graduated, she didn't even attend commencement! I had no idea what would come next for her, but our relationship was too strained for me to get an answer. Then, out of the blue, when she told us she was going to attend the MFA program at the University, well, we were so relieved. Yes, it was film, but she'd be at our alma mater. So, it felt like a connection."

"Wait—you both attended the University?"

"That's where we met! We're still very involved. I was the northeast regional director for the Alumni Association for several years. So, yes, we were pleased that Stacy would be continuing the legacy. And then when Gary decided to go there, to be close to Stacy—well, we thought we were all on the road to reconnecting. At least with Gary, we'd get updates. He was a lifeline for us. And now, both of them. I just . . . " She paused and brought her hand to her mouth, covering it as if afraid to spill out more thoughts. Her eyes were unfocused and wandering, in search of a map to a recognized port. William's phone rang and, looking at the number, he reached over and grasped Audrey's forearm.

"Yes, Doctor. This is William." He stood and listened; his face was stern and pale. He gave a curt nod, then listened some more. His face tremored slightly. "Yes, we will come right up." He quietly ended the call, handling the phone as if it were delicate glass. He looked at Audrey with a stiff formality, and she stood as well, directly across from him. "He's passed." Tears ran down his face, but his stoical expression held firm. "We have to go back up."

Audrey stood still and erect for a beat, but her composure crumbled away. Her face let go, then her body, and she deflated into William, who caught her. "My children," she said in a hoarse whisper. "My children are gone. How can this be? No, this can't be right. This is all wrong." And then she looked at something in the vague distance that only she could see, and wailed loudly, a deep, long, primal sound that passed through me like a wounded wraith. It brought me to a near panic. Others in the cafeteria looked on with quiet reverence. Some gazed down. I stood and reached out to place a hand on each of them. We remained there, the three of us, touching.

Chapter Twenty

I'm a destroyer of families. That was the only thought my brain could
hold as I wandered the streets outside of the hospital. I had stayed
with Stacy's parents until they had the fortitude to return to intensive
care and view Gary's corpse and sign documents. We parted at the elevators,
a final, salutary wave from William as the doors closed; Audrey, staring at
the floor, was catatonic. As was I, standing there in a lost, gaping slouch.
I was broken from my stupor when an impatient voice asked me if I was
getting on. I trance-walked into an elevator, and my pushy travel-mate,
scanning the expression on my face, inched to the farthest corner of the
elevator and tried to become invisible.

I couldn't shake Audrey's wail. As I wandered aimlessly, I still felt the
vibrations of it humming in me, centered in the pit of my abdomen like
a straining fist. My fortitude and resolve had been decimated. The effort
to carry on the façade—to hide behind the rationalizing curtain in which
I had draped myself—had dropped away. Now I walked about, a hollow
ghost, without navigation or purpose. Exhausted, I stopped at a bench and
sat. *Should I call McIntyre now? Show up at a precinct and confess all? Maybe
I'll just wait here on this bench until they come to me, which, at some point,
they inevitably will.* I thought of the dialogue from *Double Indemnity* as

Fred MacMurray and Barbara Stanwyck set their criminal plan in motion, ordained by fate to be their ruin: *straight down the line*. That was me now. I had gone straight down the line to my end, sitting on a bench, drained of the will to survive. Defeated by a wail.

I shut my eyes and returned to the illusion of Stacy. I still couldn't process the whole event, an acknowledgment that deepened my surrender. Had I, on some level, sensed that it was all a false narrative, a performance? There was a nagging voice in the back of my mind, but it had been mumbling and weak. Like me. She could have played any role, really. If what Audrey said was true, Stacy was likely capable of picking a performance and creating a reality. Was this latest performed character meant exclusively for me? How could she have known it would play right into my rut? An outsider, a critic of the University, a person who knew they didn't belong to the club. She was an external manifestation of all that I was feeling. A perfect ruse by a confidence artist. But how? Was it planned or improvised? Was I so pathetically transparent that she could mirror my petty complaints with such ease, lead me around on a leash? I was an idiotic lamb led to the slaughter, where she would, for God knows what reason, "break" me of my ruminations. Well, that hadn't worked out so well.

As I pondered this ultimate humiliation, it sparked a tiny flame of anger, one that demanded fanning. Was any of this really my fault? Perhaps, in my guilty state, I was missing her culpability in all that transpired; it had clouded my vision. Yes, I was devastated to see the pain her parents were going through. Their grief had derailed me, but I could not lose sight of the chain of events here. When you think about it, I had been targeted. I hadn't invited this attack. I certainly had no desire to be broken by anyone, let alone by a fabricated person who had conned me by design. *To hell with this*, I thought. I refused to succumb. Sure, I felt incredible grief for Audrey and William; they both seemed like decent people. But perhaps I empathized with them so strongly because we had all suffered at the hands of Stacy's delusional and manipulative actions. Was it not true that we were, the three of us, bonded by this fact, that we were all victims of her cruel performance? And Gary—well, he shouldn't have stood by. No, he seemed to know that she was up to something. He was an accomplice of sorts, that smirking, pompous poseur.

The truth was becoming clear: Gary and Stacy had attacked me. They were born members of the University, the elite and privileged entities who coveted and protected this institution and its legacies, and they had attacked me. Stacy, through her malicious games, had threatened my place among them. I had been targeted and groomed for expulsion. Yes, it was given that I had married into it. Perhaps I hadn't entered its walls in the conventional way, through the good fortune of lineage. My parents weren't important alumni from New Canaan. But I'd be damned if I was going to be robbed of my place because of the sabotaging actions of one of its chosen. No, I would not succumb; I would keep my place in the Village. I was not a prisoner, after all. I was in the tenured class, the true elite of the University. And I would continue to do whatever was necessary to protect my place.

As I stood from the bench with a new resolve fueled by survival, my phone rang. McIntyre, calling again. Fine. I was ready to face my adversary. I answered the call.

"Coffee?" said Detective Jackson, the name of McIntyre's bemused partner, as I'd come to learn. I was at their home precinct voluntarily, answering questions with the secure confidence of an innocent man, buoyed by my newfound sense of victimhood. It hadn't taken them long to determine I was in my building when Gary died, and, despite telling McIntyre on the phone that I'd not seen Gary, he asked if I could come in, answer some of their questions.

Playing the man with nothing to hide, I said I would be happy to, though I didn't know how much help I could be. We were in a room that parodied every interrogation room I'd seen in every cop movie: bad lighting, peeling paint, and a plain wooden table covered in etched acts of resistance. Among the many initials and profanities scratched into the wood was, resonantly, a lopsided smiley face. The greenish color of the walls was a shade only found in prisons, public schools, and hospitals. The room even had a mirror—two-way, I assumed. I was alone with Jackson, but I knew McIntyre, after excusing himself and making a quick exit, was behind the mirror, watching me and seething.

"Sure, thanks—black is fine."

"Yeah, so," Jackson said in a singsong voice. "What a clusterfuck, right? I mean, man—taking the leap the next freaking night! Dude didn't even give you all a chance to, you know, process. That was harsh."

"I'm still kind of shocked. And yes, I can't really process it. Any of it."

"Does it give you the willies knowing you were sitting in your office while Fallis was up on the roof, like, literally right above you, getting ready for his final sign-off? That would sit hard with me. Not easy to shake that, you know what I'm saying?"

"Trust me, it's been hard to not think about that."

"I mean, he may have come by to see you—I know you said he didn't, but he could have been thinking about it. Maybe that's why he was in the building. He could have been outside your damn door! It was shut, right?"

"Yes."

"You don't keep it open? You know, in case students come by?"

"Sure, during office hours, but at that hour, never. I was writing and no one was planning on coming by, as far as I knew. I didn't have any appointments, that is."

"Sure, sure. I get that. Private time. So, you never saw him?"

"As I've said, no. That's something I certainly would have recalled. Look, I'm not sure how much more helpful I can be. It's late, I'm exhausted. And, frankly, I should be home with my wife. This is really a terrible set of events, and I imagine things are not going to be easy on campus tomorrow."

"No doubt, no doubt. Hey, one more thing. Your colleague, Professor Spiers?"

Spiers. Shit. Of course; I should have known Jackson would have some card to play, out of the blue. I'd seen this scene before—the cop's friendly banter about to conclude, and a last attempt to trip up the suspect. Well,

I would keep my cool. But Spiers—he could be a problem, even as senile as he was.

"Yes, his office is down the hall from me. I saw him earlier this evening," I said.

"Yeah, looks like you were the only two up there. Cameras show him leaving before you." He scratched his chin and smiled. "I've got to say it, man: what is up with him? I don't mean to offend, but he is one strange character. You ever been to his place? Total pack rat. Thick with smoke. No fun for me, too, since I quit smoking a year ago. I was going to call the fire department, no lie."

"Yes, he is, ah, eccentric."

"Reminds me of that creepy old dude from *Phantasm*. You know that one? You're a movie guy, right?

"Sure—Angus Scrimm. That's the actor who played the Tall Man in the *Phantasm* films. A horror movie icon."

"That's right! The Tall Man." He said it slowly, drawing it out. "Scared the crap out of me back then. Well, that's kind of Spiers, you know what I mean? All in black, too. Creepy dude. Well, anyway, he said you were carrying piles of paper towels from the bathroom. That right?"

"Yes, it is. The rain had gotten in the window—I hadn't fully closed it and it was blowing right in."

"Yeah, I figured something like that. It was raining hard as shit earlier." He paused and looked around the room, landing briefly on the mirror.

"Well, as I said, I'm wiped out," I said, stifling a yawn. "I'm available if you have more questions at some point, but I think I'm done for tonight. I don't have much left in me."

"Sure, sure. We appreciate you coming by, given everything. I hope you get some rest." He sauntered to the door and opened it. "It's a damn shame, these kids killing themselves today—it's a damn epidemic."

I mumbled an affirmation and we made our way out of the room. As I left, I saw McIntyre standing in the hallway, at a distance. He glared at me. I gave a quick wave. He glared some more. I made my way around the corner and down the stairs, back out onto the street, past uniformed

police and tired-looking men and women in civilian clothes. I was happy
to get out. That last bit of questioning had almost knocked me off balance.
I still didn't think they had anything substantial, but they did have their
bloodhound sense. And they were sniffing hard.

Jackson worried me more than McIntyre. He was clearly the sharper
one, with his disarming manner and casual charm. Would they try to
get into my office? They'd need a search warrant for that. Could they get
one? Seemed unlikely to me, but what did I know? I'd been stumbling
around like an idiot in the dark. Gary's blood was smeared everywhere
in my office—and the paper towels. That's something Jackson picked
up on. *But why would they suspect me? I'm just a professor.* Yes, there was
the coincidence of proximity, but why wouldn't there be? He was a
major in my department; it was his building, too. Where else would he
have jumped from—the Business School? No, they were just following
protocol. I couldn't possibly be some lead suspect. These were suicides,
obviously. They were cousins, and very close—of course it made sense that
he would do something desperate.

I tried to shake it off as I made my way home, but the threat lingered
in the air, keeping me on edge. As I walked, it occurred to me that I
had class in the morning. Nope—not happening. I paused on the street
and accessed the course site on my phone, then sent an email out to the
class, cancelling tomorrow's session. I added some lines about support
and resources on campus, blah, blah. I slipped my phone away, ignoring
the large number of emails in my inbox, and made my way back home. I
thought about Gary's blood.

Chapter Twenty-One

Abbie was in the living room, where I'd left her, asleep on the couch. I sat quietly in the adjacent chair and looked at her. Her stillness, my stillness, the dark room—it was the most peace I'd found in days. On closer inspection, her face looked restless and strained, as if the act of unconsciousness took concentrated effort. I was struck by how beautiful she was; I knew this, of course, but in that moment, it startled me anew.

Stacy had wanted to follow in Abbie's footsteps. Of course she had. She had read her work at Choate. I'm sure it was on many a syllabus. I thought back to Stacy's bedroom and the two books—mine and Abbie's—with the box placed on top, and that picture of Stacy—so strange at the time, but clear to me now, a photo of the real Stacy, the Anastasia described by Audrey. The way it was arranged: it was like some strange altar, one whose meaning was as elusive as Stacy's reason for targeting me. It wasn't lost on me that my book was on the bottom of the stack. *Christ—movie credits*. Only in academe would this be a publishable topic. Had I chosen it as an act of satire? Was early evidence of my disdain to be found in my seminal work, my single book? Probably. I wondered if I now had it in me to write something substantive, something with crossover appeal. *Why not*, I thought—*who doesn't love movies?* Maybe this time I'd, you know, get past the credits and actually write about films. Why had I wasted all this time? I could have made my mark by now.

I got up from the chair as quietly as I could and went to the kitchen, got some water from the sink, and skimmed my emails. One caught my eye; the subject line read "Candlelight Vigil." I opened it and read. It was from a student named Alexandra Hanson, who identified herself as the vice president for student wellness policy on the undergraduate student council. It was an invitation to speak at a vigil on the campus green, to be held tomorrow evening. The council wanted me to say some words about Stacy and Gary and the loss to the community. They were asking me because of the clear commitment and dedication I had to students and to the importance of intervention. While some senior members of the administration were speaking, they felt my words would mean the most to the attending students, since the loss was a personal one for me, and because "I got it."

Oh, yes—I got it. Normally, I'd be as likely to speak at a candlelight vigil as to pull out my own teeth with pliers, but I found myself completely arrested by the idea. It felt right, almost logically forgone, like I needed to do this—I was even excited to speak. Perhaps this was penance of sorts through which I could climb my way back to my place in the University; another act of contrition—not for Stacy and Gary, but for my disrespect, my willful blindness to the gifts bestowed on me: my marriage, my job, my tenure. I let Alexandra know that I would be honored to participate. I immediately retrieved my iPad and went into the bedroom, where I started jotting down ideas for my speech.

I looked up from my notes and out from the lectern. I was front and center on the makeshift platform that served as the stage for the vigil. Hundreds of candles flickered across the campus green, making it look like a clear and starlit evening sky fallen to Earth. Most attendees were standing, but a row of folding chairs in the front held members of the student council and certain faculty and guests. William and Audrey Mann were in attendance, nattily dressed in muted colors. Both maintained their stoical, almost haughty, composure. Audrey was no longer in a stupor; she wore her public face, the practiced look of a VIP at donor events, charity auctions, and alumni reunions. Roger Croup and his child bride were there; he was crying while she comforted him with a patting hand and soft kisses on his wet cheek.

Paul sat with Abbie. Both looked at me like stunned parents, uncertain what would transpire. Paul fidgeted in his seat, and his hands tapped away on his legs. Abbie stared at me with something akin to wonder and a query: *Who is this man impersonating my husband?* Behind the row of chairs and among the standing crowd, I spotted Greta, perhaps a bit drunk, waving her candle like a groupie at a rock concert. Sitting on the stage were the University chaplain, who had opened the event with an ecumenical prayer invoking God, Allah, Buddha, and Nature; the provost of the University, his frog-like face held impassively; and Alexandra, who was serving as an emcee of sorts and introduced the speaker in a plaintive, irritating voice. I cleared my throat and began.

"Thank you, Alexandra, for this opportunity to share with you all, on this tragic occasion, as we come together as a community to give heed to the pain of losing two cherished students. As most of you know, Stacy Mann was my teaching assistant this semester. In truth, I only met her a few days ago, though it feels like I've known her much longer. I felt a bond with Stacy from the moment she walked into my office to introduce herself. That bond is even stronger now. We shared a love of film—that became quickly evident, and in the short time I knew her, I think we delved into more movie trivia than I have during weeks of teaching one of my classes."

Some respectfully muted laughter and sniffles floated up from the crowd.

"Her enthusiasm was simply contagious. She had one great passion: making films. Stacy was a doer. I talk about films; she was busy making them. And Stacy was also passionate about, well, everything." Some nods, some sad smiles. "She wasn't shy about letting you know her mind, that's for sure." Laughter, a few sniffled sobs. "And wasn't that passion contagious? I know it was for me." I paused and looked down at my notes.

"Gary, too, was not afraid to speak his mind—and what a mind, indeed: erudite, knowledgeable, and so often on point. I could always count on Gary to propel our class discussions to a higher level of inquiry. He was not afraid of controversy, and he went where his intellect would take him. It was really something to witness. I am so grateful to him for making me work harder, for making me rise to the challenge. And having had the opportunity to meet Audrey and William Mann, Stacy's parents and Gary's aunt and uncle, only makes me feel that I know Stacy and Gary even more deeply."

I turned with a gesture to Audrey and William. "What a testament they were to you both. You shared with me that Gary was more like a son to you—more like a younger brother to Stacy. Their bond and their love, fostered so well by you, will never be forgotten. I cannot begin to understand the grief and loss you must feel in having to say goodbye to the both of them, but perhaps there is some consolation, some beauty, that these two cousins, so close in life, did not spend much of it apart from each other, and now never will."

Okay, that last part came off a bit differently than I intended. I shuffled more notes, and realized I was uncertain of my place in the speech. I looked up and saw Abbie and was surprised to see tears on her face. Paul, next to her, was looking down at unusually still hands. I scanned over to Audrey and William. She was staring at me so intensely, with such focused energy, it frightened me, though I could not look away. But then I had a dawning realization as I locked into her: that intensity was fervent gratitude. Her face radiated a joyful glow. She needed this. The University was her church, her sacred ground. I was the sermonizing priest, and this was the catharsis needed, not just for her, but for all. And, I realized with epiphanic wonder, this was my church, too. I hadn't been simply fighting to stay; I was here by natural right. I belonged.

Suddenly, I was overwhelmed by it all. The sense of oneness with all present, the serenity of knowing, intrinsically and with complete certainty, that this was my time. I looked again at Abbie and she looked back with an expression that I don't think I'd ever seen, as least not directed at me. There was love, yes, and support. But the remarkable thing was the look of respect. My eyes welled and I nodded to her slightly. This, I now knew, was the answer to all of my ruminations, my self-involved musings and questions, my search for meaning behind all I did not know. This was where my stumbling path was meant to lead me, to this moment: my apotheosis, the realization of my resurrection, my union with my community, my home, my University. I put my notes to the side.

"I have some more prepared remarks, but I can't go on with them. I simply can't." I wiped my face and looked out at the glimmering candles. "All I can think about right now, looking out at you all, is how I failed. How I failed Stacy and Gary, how I failed you, my community. I can't help but feel responsible for the loss of them both. And, as hard as this is to say, we all played a part in this failure. We all let them down.

"How can that be? Because we do not stand apart. We are all connected, joined in the good and, yes, the bad. I get it—depression is real; it leads to terrible acts that steal away the people we love. Any community of this size is bound to lose someone to this terrible disease, I've been told. My rational brain gets that. But as I look out at you all—your commitment, your empathy, your grief—I know we, the University, can do better. We can do better because we are the wonderful exception. Sadly, it takes a tragic loss like this to get us to realize this point. It did for me.

"The University is an exceptional community; it always has been and always will be. We strive more deeply for greatness, examine more thoughtfully, and—yes—we care more deeply. We all must, if we are not going to let this great tradition down. And that cannot be an option." The hushed crowd was eerily quiet and looked on with shared intensity. It brought me back to that stillness in time I experienced with Stacy; she hanging from the door, finally still in death, and I staring up at her. It was like that now. Perfect stillness, perfect timelessness. I let it linger a bit more, then continued.

"I want you all to share a pledge with me, one that will make the loss of Stacy and Gary have meaning and purpose. Let us never stand apart from one another. Let us never sever the bonds connecting us all within this campus. We are a joined community; we did not enter it lightly, but with work, persistence, originality, and intelligence. We are the exceptional, and that privilege brings responsibility beyond the norms of the average, this gift we all share.

"Pledge with me now that no member of our community will stand apart, will be passed over. We will all do what we can to carry those around us who stumble. We will move forward; the University will move forward. We will not leave behind the loss of Stacy and Gary. We carry them with us, and they—in their presence—inspire us forward. For my part, this is the only path, the only redemption I can find to address my responsibility for losing them."

I choked on the last word and had to pause. Some in the audience gave cheers of support. Someone shouted: "We love you, Professor Waite." I suspected it was Greta. "This is hard," I said, and gave a sad smile and continued. "Let us never forget Stacy and Gary; let us all leave here on the same path, as one community, as one university, forward together." I paused and scanned the crowd. "Thank you. Thank you for sharing this community with me. I cherish you all." As I returned to my seat, the applause and cheers welled from the audience. The chaplain put a hand on my shoulder and whispered, "That was beautiful." Alexandra, back at the podium and barely holding it together, thanked the speakers and the attendees and said something about support and spaces, but at that point, I wasn't listening to her, and the crowd was breaking up.

I made my way to Audrey and William, shook his hand and hugged her warmly. She squeezed me with surprising strength. "Thank you," she said in my ear. "Thank you so much for this."

As I broke from her, people started to gather around me, thanking me for my words and commending me with handshakes and pats. Roger was on the periphery, holding up a power fist meekly as he sobbed. Someone behind me placed a warm, flat hand on my back and held it there, and I turned to find Abbie standing close. We looked into each other's eyes and said nothing; we didn't need to. We both understood now. I brought her in to me, and we hugged firmly and for a long time, breathing in unison, the tension in our bodies dancing away like the many flickering lights. Those around, sensing a deeper meaning, kept a respectful distance.

I finally looked up and saw Paul, a warm smile on his uncharacteristically still face. I took it all in: groups huddled together, talking, hugging, crying, supporting one another. And then, quite a distance away, beyond several clusters of conjoined people, I thought I caught a very brief glimpse of Detective Jackson, expression still bemused as he disappeared into the crowd like a spectral figure, leaving me questioning whether I had imagined his presence.

I held Abbie more tightly; I wasn't out of the woods yet. I still had my office to consider, all those traces of Gary embedded everywhere, waiting to be swabbed. And Jack Spiers. And there must be other lingering strands, out there and waiting to be uncovered. But I wasn't worried, not truly. They would not stand in my way. I knew that now. Matters would be dealt with, as one would deal with any other petty, administrative nuisance; they were tasks, no more than that. I continued to hold Abbie firmly, ideas circling my mind and joy radiating from my heart, as I basked in the knowledge that, after groping in the dark for so very long, I had finally made my way home.

Epilogue

"So, how was it? I see you got the requisite sunburn." Paul sat across from me in the faculty dining room. "And you've returned to a late Indian summer. Did you decide to bring Santa Monica back with you?"

"Right? Christ, it's warmer here than it was in California. Crazy." I nibbled at my salad.

"But you and Abbie had a good time?" he asked.

"We actually did. We slipped out from the conference whenever we could—or I should say, when she could. Abbie's always in demand, so it wasn't easy at times to get away from the clamor. But we did it, and I have to say, we had a lot of fun. And staying here didn't make sense, given everything. It's not as if the office would've been ready before we got back."

"Welcome to my building, neighbor! Look, you're lucky we had the space to accommodate you and the others, given the shortage. I still can't believe it, though how could I not believe it—it was so inevitable. How often did you all joke about this? Daily, I imagine!"

"It's kind of fitting, you know what I mean? Maybe this was his plan all along. Maybe he decided that, if his long-awaited return to being chair wasn't going to happen, he would go down in flames and take the department with him—well, some of the sixth-floor offices, at any rate."

"Right—or maybe he just dozed off with cigarette in hand and burned the place down, like everyone said he would. But your posters! I know how devastating it was to lose them. But really, how could everyone be so stupid, to allow this to go on so long. That old wood paneling on your floor was like dry kindling."

"Yeah, my posters. It hurts to think about them. Especially my signed *Casablanca*. Oh well. Abbie said I'd never straighten out my office. I guess Spiers heard her, decided to step in."

Paul chuckled and bit into his sandwich.

"What a way to go," he said. "And to run out of his office, spreading the flames. Did he have to pull a Miss Havisham and land right at your door? That's where they found him, right? That's not apocryphal?"

"Nope—that's where they found his remains. Well, it probably consumed him rapidly and he had nowhere to go but out. You think I'm a pack rat? You should've seen his office. Those piles of paper, it must have been an instant bonfire in there."

"And that pathetic sprinkler system. Like a mouse pissing on a volcano. And, of course, Facilities is saying it must have been tampered with or vandalized somehow. Oh no, it couldn't be lack of upkeep, given the wonderful job they do around campus!"

"Oh, is that what they're saying? It's natural, I suppose. A lot of liability there."

"Indeed! Well, he went out dramatically. Jack did that, at least. And, frankly, I suspect that he died a long time ago. That smoky creature in black walking around was his ghost, trapped in departmental politics." Paul tapped the table. "Are you having dessert?" We both scooted our chairs back and joined the queue at the dessert bar.

"This is where we used to part!" Paul said, as we strolled under the brilliant warm sun.

"That's right—now we have more time to gossip." The warmth encompassed me in a hug; I welcomed the sweat and heat. "So, are you going to lend me any Armenian folk art, or what? My office is bare except for my German *Goldfinger* poster. I did pick up another one, so I'll hang it today."

"I'm not sure folk art is the right aesthetic for you. And maybe you should do austere for a while, see how it fits you." We passed a group of students who waved at me and voiced hearty greetings. "Still the celebrity with students, I see," Paul said. "Are you really going to chair the student wellness taskforce? Maybe you should include fire risk on the agenda."

"Yes, of course I am! You know I'm committed to it, after everything. I think we can do a lot of good this year. You know, strike while the coals are hot, implement some real change for once."

Paul looked at me incredulously.

"Who are you and what have you done with my friend Daniel?" he said. "Speaking of student wellness, tell Abbie I'm sorry to hear about her assistant—what's his name again?"

"Terry Rockford."

"Right. To leave her in the lurch like that, with no warning. What is it with these fragile students? You simply can't get good help anymore!"

"Ha! Now, now." We entered the lobby and made our way to the elevator. "We really don't know the details of what happened, why the sudden leave of absence. It's funny, though, he seemed fine the last time I talked to him." I pressed the up button. "I hope it wasn't something I said."

"Oh, please—you're so deferential you'd have trouble driving flies away." We rode silently, then got off the elevator.

"All right, I'd better do some work for tomorrow's class," I said.

"Finishing with *Psycho*?"

"Yep. I'm lecturing on one of my favorite parts: Norman's monologue during the final scene. Well, Norman's mother, really. Norman's fully eclipsed by her at that point. Funny piece—you know it; the jailed Mrs. Bates knows she's being watched, so she's being meek as a lamb; she says, 'I'm not even going to swat that fly!' The famous final gaze into the camera—I love that; always creeps out the students."

"Anthony Perkins is so wonderfully campy. Friend of Dorothy, of course. Well, off you go; get to it. Knock on my door when you're leaving for the day."

I unwrapped the framed poster and propped it on the table against the wall, across from my desk. It was very good quality for an early print—the colors had hardly faded at all. *Deliverance*. The second design. The extended arms pointing the rifle, reaching out of—or sinking into—the waters. I planned to have some more posters framed. I'd already ordered an excellent first print of *The Exorcist*. I owed her that much.

I went to my desk and sat down. As was becoming my daily habit, I opened my desk drawer, reached to the back, pulled out the silver Zippo lighter, and traced the JS initials with my finger. Stupid to keep it, especially in the office. I'd find a safe place for it; but I found I simply couldn't get rid of it. To do so almost seemed sacrilegious, profane. Disrespectful to Jack and his role in this saga. I put it back in the drawer and closed it. Better do some work.

I moved some papers to the side and placed Oliver Stone on top of them: the solitary survivor from my office, cleansed of ash and blood, of any trace of the task it had performed. Jackson and McIntyre could still buzz around me, but there would be no fly-swatting from me. I'd follow Mrs. Bates's example. And what would be the point, anyway? What could they do? Let them have their suspicions—their convictions, even. I was safe for now. Purged clean by fire. They remained on the outside, and I was out of reach, protected by the borders of the Village. I lived here. They were merely occasional visitors, permitted a day pass from the outside.

I looked out the window. Not as good a view as from my old office, but I could still see part of the campus green, students and faculty coming and going on the paths. I turned my attention back to the *Deliverance* poster across from me and, settling in the chair and shifting my gaze to a blank spot on the wall to its left, welcomed the descent into my fugue state, into the belly of my sweet deliverance.

My phone rang, dispelling my hour-long reverie. I looked at the screen and recognized the number. A smile of genuine warmth spread across my face and I answered.

"Detective McIntyre!" I said cheerfully. "I've been expecting your call."

The End